COUNTERFEIT TRAIL

Counterfeit money is flooding into Texas, brought in by the beautiful, elusive ex-Civil War spy, Marie Madelaine. When Treasury detective Eli Johnson is murdered, Texas Ranger Brad Saunders, assisted by the raw young sheriff of Queensville, is left to follow a trail of deception on a grand scale. Not only is the Texan economy under threat, but also the future of Revolutionary General Porfirio Diaz, whose army is assembling to overthrow the Mexican government. With a hundred thousand dollars in counterfeit money at stake, Brad pits his wits against Colonel Carlos Valdez, who owes allegiance to no man but himself.

COUNTERFEIT TRAIL

COUNTERFEIT TRAIL

by

D. A. Horncastle

Dales Large Print Books
Long Preston, North Yorkshire,
BD23 4ND, England.

British Library Cataloguing in Publication Data.

Horncastle, D. A.
    Counterfeit trail.

    A catalogue record of this book is
    available from the British Library

    ISBN   1-84262-489-X pbk
    ISBN   978-1-84262-489-0 pbk

First published in Great Britain in 1994 by Robert Hale Limited

Published in Large Print 2006 by arrangement with
Robert Hale Ltd.

Dales Large Print is an imprint of Library Magna Books Ltd.

Printed and bound in Great Britain by
T.J. (International) Ltd., Cornwall, PL28 8RW

*For
Julie*

ONE

In the upstairs room of the barber shop Dan Jasper lay bound and gagged on the bed. The elderly barber was dying slowly by asphyxiation. Two Mexicans, their sombreros pulled low over their eyes, squatted on their heels with their backs to the adobe walls. Thin blue spirals of smoke twirled upwards from their thin cigars as they watched Dan's death throes with callous indifference.

Equally indifferent, Colonel Carlos Valdez of the Mexican Revolutionary Army crouched beside the half-open window in the upper storey of the barber shop, peering through a brass bound spy glass across the street at a window at the same level in Queensville's Grand Palace Hotel. On the floor beside him lay a Winchester rifle. In the heat of the siesta, nothing stirred except the flies buzzing desultorily on the window pane while in the deserted street below a sleepy mongrel turned round twice before resuming its comfortable spot in the doorway of a general store.

Valdez drew away from the window, stood up and wiped a little trickle of sweat away from his drooping black moustache. He was a tall, well-built man dressed similarly to his companions in a short blue jacket with red and yellow facings and brown pants with gold braid down held up with a blue sash. It was the nearest thing to a uniform worn by followers of General Diaz but in essence typical of the dress worn by the bands of outlaws of Mexican extraction who infested this south westernmost corner of Texas.

Valdez took a last draw on the stub of his cigar and ground out the butt with his heel.

'Pass me the bottle,' he said. As he spoke to his *compadres*, the harshness of command was in his voice.

Without a word, one of the men leaning against the wall kicked a bottle of tequila, setting it in motion towards him across the bare floorboards. Valdez hesitated before he picked it up and drained it. With a sigh, he wiped his lips with the back of his left hand, each finger of which was adorned with a solid gold ring. Then he picked up the rifle and sighted it carefully through the open window.

The clump of boots on the stairs distracted him. He stared at the man who appeared in the doorway. Whipcord thin, unlike his *compadres* the Mexican carried no guns, only a brace of throwing knives, one on each hip.

'What is it, Garcia?' Valdez demanded.

'I have news,' the man replied. He produced a thin cigar and paused whilst he lit it. 'A ranger just rode into town.'

'Los Diablos Tejanos!' Valdez spat the words with such venom, it almost roused the interest of the two men slumped beside the wall. 'But why did you not follow him?'

'I did. He went into the hotel. I spoke with one of the maids. After a little persuasion she told me he is with Senor Johnson...'

Valdez snatched up his spy-glass and resumed his watch at the window. The light was behind him, making his task easier. Inside the room he detected the shadowy outline of two men.

'So, my friend, you have called in the rangers,' he muttered.

Garcia fished in his pocket and withdrew a silver pocket watch.

'Colonel, the stage is due two hours from now. We cannot wait here much longer.'

Valdez ignored him as he stayed for some time, holding the spy-glass steady as he focussed it on the window of the room. Suddenly he laid it down, picked up the Winchester and took aim.

11

'Get ready to leave.' His cheek touched the cold metal of the weapon and his forefinger curled round the trigger. 'We will deal with the ranger later,' he said softly.

The man sitting behind the desk looked up from the chess board as Brad Saunders entered the room. His glance, delivered with a slight turn of his bald-domed head, reminded Brad of the keen appraisal of a hawk hovering in search of prey.

The man paused, a pawn held between the first two fingers of his right hand. He put down the piece and pushed the chess board carefully to one side.

'You're five minutes early, Ranger Saunders.'

He rapped out the words in the crisp, hard-edged tone of voice of the Easterner. Brad did his best to conceal his natural feeling of aversion. Although the war was finished ten years now, he still hadn't yet learned to rub shoulders easily with men he'd fought against in that bitter conflict.

After they had shaken hands, the man indicated a chair for Brad and eased all five foot two of himself back into his own.

'Now I guess you're wondering what a New Yorker is doing out here in Texas?' he said with a wry smile.

'All I know is your name is Eli Johnson,' Brad drawled. 'Captain McNelly instructed me to meet with you here in Queensville and to assist you in your investigation.'

Johnson gave a curt nod. 'I guess you've no idea what it's all about?'

When Brad shook his head, Johnson gave a sigh of relief. 'Good. Back in Austin, the Governor said Captain McNelly could be relied on to keep his mouth shut.' He stroked his bushy black Burnsides thoughtfully as he shot a penetrating glance at Brad.

Brad eased into the leather backed chair. Luxury! It was the first soft seat he'd sat on after a week of hard riding from the hinterland of Texas. He'd left Blaze, his big bay stallion, in the care of a Mexican youth at the livery barn in the side street and hurried across the plaza to the hotel without even pausing to slake his thirst. The salty tang in the air and the gulls wheeling over the boats moored in the tiny fishing harbour were a sharp reminder that the vastness of the Lone Star State ended right here on the Gulf of Mexico.

In the presence of this dapper little man, dressed in a plain grey suit, white shirt and black string tie, Brad felt acutely conscious that his own riding boots and buckskin trousers were smothered in trail dust. Under his open vest, his grey flannel shirt was stained with sweat. His cheeks bristled with stubble for he hadn't had time to call in at old Dan Jasper's barber shop over the way to pay his respects. The only part of him that felt comfortable was the Single Action Army Model Peacemaker strapped to his right hip. In truth, he looked every inch a tough border outlaw. His uncompromising image had its advantages – and its disadvantages. On the one hand only a fool would dare to cross him when he was riding the trail; on the other, it was little wonder the lobby clerk had glanced twice at him before letting him into the hotel.

He glanced about him. After the heat and dust of the journey, the atmosphere in here was pleasantly cool. The carpeted room was the anteroom of the best suite in the Grand Palace Hotel. That name wasn't pretentious for the floor was carpeted, a chandelier hung from the ceiling, oil paintings of western scenes hung in gilded frames from the papered walls and the solid oak furniture gleamed after a recent polish. Through the half-open window the scuffle of the hooves of a passing horse in the dusty street sounded a world away. Whoever this Eli Johnson was, he certainly travelled the country in style...

'Whiskey or beer?'

Brad settled for a bottle of beer. Johnson poured himself a generous measure of amber liquid into a cut glass tumbler from the bottle standing on a side table. He slid a tall glass and bottle of beer followed by a box of Havanas across the desk to Brad. Johnson produced a fancy silver cigar cutter; Brad sliced off the end of his with the razor sharp blade of his Bowie knife. As the two men shared a lucifer they eyed each other with the respect every man accords to another who follows a different slant to the same profession.

Brad lowered the level in his glass by half and there followed a pause until their cigars were drawing to their satisfaction. Then Johnson said, 'Ranger Saunders, what I am about to tell you is so confidential, you must not tell another living soul.'

The little man's lugubrious tone removed any sense of melodrama from his statement. Brad exhaled a smoke ring and held his counsel, watching the struggles of a solitary fly as, caught by the smoke, it strove giddily to keep its tenuous foothold on the ceiling.

'I asked Captain McNelly for the services of one of his best men,' Johnson went on.

He grimaced. 'Now I'll allow he seemed somewhat put out at that request.'

Brad wasn't surprised. The fact that McNelly hand-picked his men was common knowledge to anyone in south west Texas. To McNelly, Johnson's request would be a contradiction in terms if not an insult.

Johnson leaned forward to flick ash into a silver plated tray. It was a curiously fastidious gesture, but it in no way disturbed Brad.

'I gather you rangers are held in high esteem in Texas,' Johnson said.

'We're doin' our best, but things have gotten real bad in this part of Texas since the war,' Brad admitted. 'Law and order has broken down. But now men like McNelly are gettin' a grip on it, we'll win in the end.'

Johnson nodded. 'Well, now me, I'm in the employ of the Department of the Treasury.'

So Johnson was a Government Agent! As he paused to allow this information to sink in, Brad's face broke into a wry smile. Only one thing could bring the long arm of the U.S. Treasury as far as Queensville – *counterfeit money!*

Johnson flicked ash from his cigar with a nervous twitch of his nicotine stained fingers. 'So now I guess you know why I'm here,' he said.

'It ain't the first time someone's faked notes,' Brad replied offhandedly.

The detective nodded vigorously. 'Sure, sure, I know. In the early days, when every country bank issued its own notes, counterfeiting in a small way was commonplace. But this case is different. National Bank Notes are being counterfeited at the moment on a much larger scale. It's a big operation. My department reckons there may be as much as half a million dollars of it in circulation.'

Brad's lips pursed in a silent whistle.

'You'll appreciate that this is bad news for Texas,' Johnson continued. 'We don't want to publicise it for loss of confidence will wreck the economy. Money will become worthless and life will be even harder for all the honest men who are trying to build a life out here.'

Didn't Brad know it! He recalled how during the last desperate days of the war Confederate money had become so worthless he'd stuffed his worn out riding boots with ten-dollar bills just to keep his feet warm...

Johnson produced his wallet, withdrew a crisp new $20 note and passed it across to Brad.

'Look at this.'

Brad did as instructed, smiling wryly to himself for this single banknote represented

17

half a month's pay. He examined it closely, holding it up to the light. The wavy water-mark was clearly visible. He shook his head. 'Don't see nuthin' wrong with this,' he confessed.

Johnson smiled for the first time. 'Didn't think you would. It's legit.' He withdrew another note carefully and slid it across the desk. 'Now, what do you make of this?'

Brad held the two side by side. He smoothed them flat between his roughened fingers and as he stroked his lantern jaw, his forehead puckered into a frown of concentration as if he were a student doing an examination paper. He did all the simple checks that were part of his job. There was a serial number, the designs matched, so did the colours and signatures. The water-marks checked out.

After a few moments he shook his head, mystified.

'I've seen forged notes before, but these ... waal, they both seem OK to me.'

Johnson sat back and made a pyramid with his fingers. He was clearly enjoying himself.

'Take a look at the serial numbers,' he said.

Brad scrutinised the digits carefully. 'Nope,' he replied.

'Take a closer look,' the little man urged. 'Compare both notes.'

Suddenly it clicked. 'Seems like the numbers on this second note are a mite smaller,' Brad said, thoughtfully.

Johnson sat back with a grunt of satisfaction. 'To an experienced handler there is no detectable difference in paper texture and print quality, but there is a difference in type size on the serial numbers. In printer's parlance it's precisely one point. If I gave you a full page of each, you'd tell the difference immediately. But the serial number on a banknote is so short, the difference is virtually indistinguishable – unless you know what you're looking for and make a comparison as you've just done.'

'Very clever,' Brad muttered. He tapped the note with his forefinger. 'This must be mighty close to a perfect forgery.'

'Just so,' Johnson agreed.

Brad shook his head in wonderment. 'Got anyone in the frame for this?'

Johnson took a long drag on his cigar. He picked up a scroll and opened it to reveal a map of Texas.

'Counterfeit money has turned up here in Laredo, Eagle Pass, Sanderson and El Paso.' He stubbed, at each location on the map with his forefinger as he spoke.

'Can't you trace it back?'

Johnson shook his head. 'I've been working on this investigation for close on a year now. The money has been used in small amounts to make cattle deals. It's been accepted and traded on through several parties including banks, making it impossible to discover its origin. Some of it has gone into Mexico. We know that the *rurales* are aware of it.'

'So who's spreadin' it around? A travellin' salesman maybe?'

Johnson nodded. 'I worked on those lines for a long time but without a result. I checked every town of any size from here to El Paso but came up with nothing.' He leaned forward, his eyes gleaming with the intensity of a man dedicated to his job. 'But now I figure I've made a major breakthrough. If my theory is correct, I believe that a courier is bringing a consignment of counterfeit money to Queensville on the stage from Corpus Christi at six o'clock this evening.'

'So what do you want me to do?' Brad demanded.

'Help me with surveillance.'

Brad groaned inwardly. Had he ridden across half Texas just to play Bo-Peep for a Federal department? 'Do we know the guy we're lookin' for?' he asked.

Johnson smiled and withdrew his wallet from his inside breast pocket. He shook out a faded photograph.

As Brad looked at it, he took a sharp intake of breath and glanced back at Johnson.

The detective nodded. 'Yeah, it's a woman.'

Brad stared at the photograph. It was one of those faces once seen, never forgotten. Taken in a studio, the photographer had caught an impression of a woman whose innocent smile seemed completely at odds with her darkly watchful eyes. Brad shook his head in wonderment. Suddenly he felt the hairs stand up on the nape of his neck. Here was a woman who would ensnare a man and lead him to his doom without a trace of remorse. Instinctively he realised he'd rather tangle with a gang of outlaws.

'Who is this?' Brad asked.

'Her real name is Simone de Bau. She is the sister of the Marquis de Bau. The family emigrated from France in the fifties and built up a cotton plantation. Simone trained to be an opera singer. When the war came, the Marquis joined the Confederate Army and commanded an artillery battery. He's a real dandy. Waxed moustaches, fancy clothes, silver topped cane. But you can't go by

21

appearances, his superiors reported that he was an excellent soldier and highly thought of by his men. When the war started, Simone quit singing, changed her name to Pauline Leroy, and became a Confederate spy. Towards the end when we were closing in on her, she disappeared. We figured she'd left the country and returned to France.'

'You said "when *we* were closing in on her",' Brad said. He looked at Johnson shrewdly. 'Who's *we?*'

Johnson smiled a little sheepishly. 'Sorry, Ranger Saunders, I was forgettin' you must have fought for the Confederacy. During the war I worked as a secret agent for the North. I spent most of '64 trailin' Simone de Bau up an' down the eastern seaboard. It was my job to keep watch on her movements. I succeeded pretty well until I lost her at the end.'

Brad was silent for a moment, collecting his thoughts. Life dealt strange cards. Never for one moment would he have believed he'd end up siding against one of his own people.

'The war's been over ten years, now,' Johnson reminded him. 'We're the United States of America now.'

'Is the Marquis de Bau involved in this?'

Johnson drew heavily on his cigar. 'I believe he is.'

'Where is he now?'

'Back east. He lost his plantation during the war. Afterwards he went into ranching in Montana and failed spectacularly. But that didn't deter him, since then he's got a finger in a mighty big pie of business deals – includin' a printing works in New York where we believe the counterfeit money is being made.'

Johnson rose and walked over to the open window and stood with his back to it. A light breeze off the sea ruffled the heavy drapes. Over his right shoulder, the raucous cry of a gull, perched on a nearby roof, filled the air.

'Wherever his sister has performed, counterfeit money has appeared in the area. Not in vast quantities – five grand maybe. Usually through the criminal element who frame some innocent guy with a deal he believes is legit. It's an expensive lesson. Simone is clever – she doesn't use it herself. Now I figure that her brother is using her to pass money through to pay for cattle deals. She attracts well-heeled businessmen like a spider to her web. Her job gives her the perfect cover for this kind of operation. I'm convinced that the Marquis is plannin' some kinda deal in these parts. Now, here's what we're gonna do...'

The sharp crack of a gunshot cut off Johnson's words in mid-flow. A look of intense surprise filled the detective's face as a neat red hole appeared in the centre of his forehead. As Brad leapt to his feet, his hand forking for his Colt, Johnson toppled forward across the desk, scattering chess pieces all over the floor.

The room fell silent except for the crazed buzzing of the fly. Brad uncoiled from his seat and sprang away instinctively from the window. Years of gun fighting experience came into play as he leapt clear of the open window and flattened his back to the outer wall, his Colt held high.

As he inched along the wall towards the window, the curtains flapped gently in the breeze. Brad realised intuitively that the immediate danger was over. Looking down into the street he could see a black and white cur ambling across the Street and a couple of guys moving around in the deep shadow cast by the hotel building as if nothing had happened. Why not? The sound of a gunshot in a Texas town was a normal event in these turbulent times – and the chance of someone seeing the consequences of this particular shot were very low indeed unless they happened to be looking up at this particular hotel window at precisely the right moment.

Brad holstered his weapon and strode for the door. As he opened it, the barrel of a revolver jabbed painfully into his ribs.

'Curb your hurry, mister,' the owner said. 'You're not going anywhere right now.'

TWO

Brad's eyes travelled slowly upwards until they finally came to rest on the face of one of the biggest guys he'd set eyes on in a long time. Common sense dictated he do exactly as he was told, so he backed off, raising both hands. As he did so, he noticed the highly polished star pinned to the newcomer's elegant calf-skin vest.

'You the law round here, boy?' he asked.

'Sure – I'm Sheriff Tilson McCracken.'

Brad didn't miss the note of pride in the young man's face.

'Say, you must be Abe McCracken's boy?'

'Sure.' The youngster tossed back a mane of hair as yellow as a ripe cornfield as he scrutinised Brad. His eyes narrowed and his expression became sombre, but his big chest swelled with pride as he said, 'Pa was the best sheriff in the whole of the south west.'

The boy was right. It had happened about six months back. Abe McCracken's body had been discovered floating in the Rio Grande riddled with bullets. McNelly had assigned Ranger Miller to the investigation. A meticulous investigator, who seldom admitted defeat, the angry and frustrated Miller had returned empty-handed.

'I reckon Abe McCracken came too close to a shady cattle deal fixed by a slippery customer called Jake Rauchtenbauer,' he told Brad grimly. 'He paid for that with his life.'

But for the moment, Brad was puzzled. He seldom had to look up to a guy, but at six and a half feet tall, this kid looked formidable enough without the big Le Mat nine-shot revolver he was holding in a hand that could span a dinner plate. Yet there was a gentleness in his bearing and educated manner about the way he spoke which was completely at odds with his forceful manner. It seemed to Brad that he was acting a part he didn't suit.

'How long you been a lawman, Tilson?'

'Hold it, mister, I'll do the talking,' the youngster snapped. Still keeping a wary eye on Brad, he stooped to examine the corpse. 'Well, now, I heard the shot from down in the plaza and figured it came from here. It seems like I got my first homicide on my hands.' He looked up at Brad. 'And the culprit as well.'

'Right first, wrong second,' Brad replied. 'Listen, Tilson, I ain't got time to waste. I'm a Texas Ranger.'

'Oh yeah?'

'Let me flip open my vest and I'll show you my badge.'

'Hey, what d'you take me for, some kinda greenhorn?'

The youthful sheriff eyed Brad, suspicion rampant in his frank blue eyes.

As Brad's hand moved, he said, 'Just hold it right there, mister. I'll do the movin'.'

Brad froze as the barrel of the Le Mat came an uncompromising inch from his nose. One touch on the trigger and his life was over. The last time he'd seen a weapon like this was in the hands of Jeb Stuart and his fellow officers during the war.

'Where in the hell did you get that piece of artillery?' Brad asked the young lawman.

Tilson eyed Brad with contempt. 'Ain't no way you're gonna fool me with that kinda talk. But if it interests you, my uncle left it me when he died last year. He was a guy outa the same mould as my pa. They both served with Stonewall in the Valley. Uncle

27

Seth lost both legs at Chancellorsville – the same day that Stonewall died.'

Brad listened in silence. Wherever he went he heard a catalogue of similar harrowing stories from the war. Like a blood-red thread they were woven forever into the tapestry of American history. And now, in Tilson McCracker, he could see the next generation appearing on the frontier eager to blood themselves in fire and steel. Would they never learn?

Tilson stepped forward and flipped Brad's vest open. His eyes widened as he saw the silver star which proclaimed Brad's office.

'So you *are* a Texas Ranger!' he said incredulously.

'McNelly's Special Company,' Brad said, lowering his hands. 'Name's Brad Saunders. You only have to wire HQ in San Antonio to prove it.'

'You sure don't advertise the fact,' Tilson complained as he holstered his weapon, eyeing Brad's appearance with distaste.

Brad took in the check shirt, calf skin vest and well-cut levis the young lawman was wearing and for the third time that day was made to realise he looked like a saddle tramp. Summoning all the dignity he could muster he replied, 'It don't always pay to.'

'Say, are you guys still investigating my father's murder?' Tilson asked. 'Or have you written it off?'

'We never give up,' Brad replied. 'Sooner or later we'll catch up with him.'

'Maybe you'd better – before I do,' Tilson said darkly.

'Is this why you're a lawman?' Brad asked.

'That's my business,' Tilson replied curtly. He leaned over to inspect the bullet hole in Johnson's head. 'Looks like he's been backshot,' he remarked as he straightened up and looked cautiously out of the window.

'Right,' Brad said. He joined Tilson by the window. 'Judgin' at the angle the bullet entered his head I reckon the gun was fired from one of the windows over yonder rather than from the street.'

Tilson was mortified. 'I guess I never figured that,' he muttered. He looked back at the body. 'Somebody must have wanted him outa the way pretty bad.'

The fly suddenly landed on Johnson's face and ran lightly across his staring eyes. Suddenly Tilson's face turned a sickly pale.

'You feelin' all right, boy?' Brad asked tentatively.

Tilson turned abruptly away from him and hurried into the bedroom. Brad listened to the sound of him being violently sick – hopefully into the chamber pot.

A few minutes later the youngster emerged, the colour returning to his cheeks.

He looked at Brad shamefacedly. 'I guess you must think I'm soft,' he muttered.

Brad smiled bleakly. 'I'd have been mighty concerned if you hadn't felt that way,' he remarked. 'When the day comes I can look at a corpse without feelin' anythin' at all then it's time for me to quit.'

Brad's brow wrinkled as he surveyed the street. 'Best spot would have been yonder upper floor of the block dead opposite. There's an open window, 'bout level with this one. The sun's just right, too.'

'But, it couldn't have been from there!' Tilson exclaimed. 'That's Dan Jasper's place.'

As Brad peered out again, he caught sight of the striped pole indicating the barber shop.

Tilson shook his head. 'Naw, Dan Jasper's as straight as they come. He and his wife live over the shop.'

The boy was right. Brad had called at Dan Jasper's place a couple of times during his travels in the past. Old Dan had served as a gunner with Lee and they'd traded memories about their experiences during the war.

The killer had gone. Brad's sixth sense was

honed enough to know when danger lurked and when it didn't. He turned his attention back to Johnson's corpse. An inspection revealed he was wearing a shoulder holster with a Derringer – which was no more than he would have expected from a man in his line of work.

Under Tilson's interested gaze, Brad commenced a thorough search of the pockets of Johnson's suit, turning out his wallet, pocket watch, a box of lucifers, a pencil, a few nickels and dimes and a silk handkerchief with the embroidered monogram EJ.

'No identification?' Tilson asked.

Brad shook his head. A feeling of frustration rose inside him as it dawned that he was going to find out nothing more.

'I gotta have his name, at least,' Tilson persisted. 'I got paperwork to do.'

'Eli Johnson,' Brad said reluctantly. 'He worked for the government...'

As Brad withdrew Johnson's wallet, the photograph of a woman fluttered to the floor. Before Brad could move, Tilson bent down to retrieve it.

His lips pursed in a silent whistle.

'Whoa ... say, now, wait a minute...'

'D'you know her?' asked Brad tentatively.

'Sure I do.' Tilson tapped the photograph

with his forefinger. 'Why, this is Marie Madelaine! Her face is on bills posted all over town. She gonna be singing over at the Black Joke Saloon.'

Brad stared at the photograph. *Simone de Bau, Pauline Leroy, Marie Madelaine...*

'The Black Joke? Who owns that place?'

Tilson shrugged. 'Guy called Jake Rauchtenbauer.'

Jake Rauchtenbauer!

'Know anythin' 'bout him?' Brad asked casually.

The tall young sheriff shrugged his broad shoulders. 'He rode into town about three months back. Word is he was once involved with rustling on the Rio Grande, but now it seems he's goin' straight. Before he came, the old Wayfarer Saloon was clapped out. Rauchtenbauer bought it for a song, spent money on it and renamed it the Black Joke. He hired a few high class saloon gals who know how to be discreet and with singers like Marie Madelaine comin' to perform he's sittin' in clover now.'

From the way he spoke, it was obvious that Jake Rauchtenbauer was no friend of Tilson's. But it was also plain enough to Brad that he knew nothing of Ranger Miller's suspicions.

Tilson's eyes dwelt on the picture. 'All the guys are wild about her comin' here. Oh boy, don't she take a real fine photograph?'

Brad threw him a half-amused glance. 'Sounds like you've taken a shine fer her, too.'

The youngster flushed. 'Naw, I guess she's a mite too old for the likes of me.' He looked at Brad quizzically. 'How come this guy has her picture? Was he married to her or somethin'?'

Brad smiled ironically as he took the photograph back.

'Say, d'you mind tellin' me what this is all about?' Tilson asked him.

Brad thought for a moment. The temptation to tell the young sheriff the little he already knew was great, but his innate caution prevented him from doing so. He'd lay his cards down when he was good and ready, and not before.

'Not right now,' he said. 'That ain't no disrespect to you, Tilson, but Johnson gave me certain information in strictest confidence. You gotta trust my judgement – OK?'

Tilson shrugged. 'That's fine by me. But what about next of kin?'

'Leave that with me,' Brad replied. 'I'll have to make a report to Captain McNelly.

No reason why you shouldn't get the coroner's report and then have him buried.'

'Fine. But if you need any help...'

'Let's you and me go check out Dan Jasper's place. There just might be a few clues,' Brad said. 'We'd better inform the management on the way down.'

As they passed through the hotel lobby, Tilson paused and gave instructions to the clerk to contact the mortician and notify the County Coroner.

Brad and Tilson left the hotel and set out across the tree enclosed plaza. As they reached the centre, Brad's attention was drawn to a small group of horsemen gathered in the deep shadow of a side street alongside the Queensville County Bank. There were four of them. The sun highlighted red and gold braid on their blue jackets and dun coloured pants as they emerged into the sunlit plaza.

'Guess they are some of General Diaz' men,' Tilson remarked. 'His camp's only about two hours' ride west from here.'

An innate sense of suspicion forewarned Brad of danger and even as the riders urged their horses into a gallop, his right hand was darting for his Colt and within seconds he was hitting the ground, firing, rolling over and over and finally curling into a ball to avoid the flying hooves of the horses and the hail of bullets which swept the sidewalks and sent the terrified citizens of Queensville scurrying for cover.

As he fired, Brad became aware of the great boom of another weapon alongside him. To his intense relief, he saw Tilson, belly-down, alongside him in the dust, triggering his big Le Mat for all he was worth at the four riders retreating from them. Brad blazed away until his weapon was empty, but he knew it was in vain. As a former cavalryman, he was well aware that the chance of hitting a prone man with a revolver shot whilst making a charge was virtually impossible. The reverse was also true.

Brad leapt to his feet and had begun instinctively to reload his weapon before he realised the impossible *had* happened; the young sheriff was lying in the dust and townsfolk were already fluttering round him like buzzards to a kill. He himself was unharmed but the sleeve of his shirt had been caught by a flying hoof and rent it open adding to his already tattered appearance.

Brad swore bitterly as he holstered his Colt and stooped over the inert body. He'd only known the kid five minutes and already he felt as responsible for him as if he were his own brother.

He arrived beside the body at the same moment as a young woman. She pushed Brad away unceremoniously, gathered her skirts and bent over Tilson.

'Leave him be!' she rapped. She looked up at the crowds gathering about her. 'Don't just stand there! Somebody get Doc Jeffries – *quickly!*'

Brad bent down to retrieve Tilson's Le Mat and backed off.

As the girl looked down at Tilson, it tore Brad up to see her eyes streaming with tears.

'Tilson, I told you not to take that sheriff's badge,' she sobbed as she spoke.

'Make way fer the Doc!'

The crowd parted to let a tall thin man slip through, His ancient black suit, frayed at the collar and cuffs gave him a raven-like appearance. But he obviously commanded the respect of the local citizenry for a hush fell over the plaza as he bent down over Tilson. After a few moments a smile creased his gaunt features.

Tilson opened his eyes and groaned.

'Is he gonna be OK, Doc?' the girl asked anxiously.

Doc Jeffries looked up, his smile revealing a row of teeth as discoloured as ancient tombstones.

'No need to worry, Miss Clayton,' he pronounced. 'I know him as well as I know you, I brought you both into the world. Slug's jest parted his hair. The boy's gonna have himself a headache fer awhile but he's strong. He'll survive.'

Under Doc Jeffries' supervision, willing hands improvised a stretcher from a blanket offered by the owner of a nearby general store, but in the event it wasn't needed, for Tilson had recovered consciousness and was already scrambling to his feet as fast as a maverick caught napping.

'Where'n the hell did those *ladrones* get to?' he muttered, looking round him in obvious bewilderment.

The girl grabbed his arm. 'Come on, Tilson, let me take you home, you need rest,' she said.

As Brad handed Tilson his Le Mat, the girl turned on him.

'Hey, you were steppin' alongside Tilson, just now. You mind tellin' me what was all that about, mister?' she demanded.

The other bystanders heard her and gathered about Brad, hostility in their eyes.

37

'You heard my daughter's question, stranger. What have you got to say for yourself?'

Brad turned to face a thick-set man in early middle age. Clean shaven apart from a neatly trimmed moustache, dressed in a light grey suit and homburg hat, he looked every inch the self-assured rancher. His demeanour was such as to convey the impression that he expected his audience to defer to him without question.

'Two pieces of gunplay in one afternoon. One man killed and another wounded,' the newcomer said. 'It's scandalous. Where's the law in this town? That's what I'd like to know.'

'We only just elected Tilson sheriff, Mr Clayton, give the boy a chance,' a man said respectfully.

'I hear you,' Joel Clayton replied. 'And now he well nigh gets himself killed. I warned everyone that this job needs an experienced peace officer, not someone still wet behind the ears.'

'You're quite right, Mr Clayton.'

The speaker was lounging against the hitching post outside the Black Joke Saloon. A heavily built man in his early thirties, like Clayton he was dressed in a suit, his thumbs hooked into his gunbelt supporting a paunch straining the buttons of his fancy red silk vest.

A skinny old-timer ejected a stream of tobacco juice. 'I reckon so, Mr Rauchtenbauer. Edification don't teach a man gunfightin',' he opined. His lower jaw dropped open, revealing a set of brown-stained teeth as he cackled with laughter. 'You mark my words, Tilson, you should've stayed with yore studies. That way you might choke to death on lemon pie when you reach three score years and ten. Why, jest look what happened to yore pa...'

The old-timer's voice turned to a hoarse croak as Tilson grabbed him by the throat.

'Hold your tongue, you old goat, or I'll...'

'Take it easy, Tilson,' Brad intervened.

'He's right,' Rauchtenbauer said contemptuously. 'Face it, McCracken, you ain't got what it takes to be a lawman.'

'Hold your tongue, Jake Rauchtenbauer!' Victoria cried.

Jake Rauchtenbauer lifted his stetson and made a mocking bow. Alert to straws in the wind, Brad marked the man and his arrogant attitude.

'It's high time we brought in the rangers,' Victoria said flatly.

Tilson wiped his hand over his bloodstained face. 'Now just hold it folks. I'm the law round here.'

'You got a ranger right here, ma'am,' Brad stepped forward as he spoke and flipped open his vest.

A low murmur ran through the crowd as they saw the silver star flash in the sunlight.

'Name's Brad Saunders, I ride with McNelly's Special Company,' he announced. As he spoke, he knew he was sacrificing his anonymity by revealing his presence.

'So just what brings you here, ranger?' As Clayton spoke, Brad noticed with a keen sense of satisfaction how the man's overbearing attitude had evaporated and that his face had turned pale under his tan. Beyond him, he caught sight of Jake Rauchtenbauer melting into the crowd.

Victoria Clayton slipped her arm through her father's.

'Ranger Saunders, can you explain this unseemly fracas just now? Why, Tilson was very nearly killed.' Her eyes were blazing with anger as she spoke.

Brad removed his hat and held her gaze calmly.

'Now, see here, Miss Victoria,' he said. As he spoke he was aware that he was speaking to an audience as well as an individual.

'Captain McNelly sent me here on a special investigation...'

'If it's about Tilson's father, it's about time you people brought his killer to justice,' Victoria interrupted heatedly.

Brad's cold glance silenced her.

'...why I'm here is my business.' His eyes swept though the audience, impressing his own legally invested authority on each and every one of them.

'Now, see here, Saunders,' Clayton said. 'You can't just barge in here and interfere in the affairs of this town without the sheriff's permission.'

Brad rounded on him. 'Clayton, just now I heard you saying how much law this town needed. As it happens the sheriff has stated quite clearly that he has no objection to me bein' here.'

He had barely finished speaking when everyone's attention was drawn to the sound of galloping hooves entering the plaza.

'Glory Hallelujah, it be the stage!' Clem Partridge exclaimed. He ejected another stream of baccy juice. 'Hank's drivin' an' by his all-fired hurry, I reckon he's bin and got hisself robbed!'

THREE

The old-timer's prediction proved accurate for the driver hauled his team of lathered and blown horses drawing the Concord stage coach to standstill. He gestured wildly towards the crowd now thronging the plaza. He was a stockily built man, with lean, sinewy forearms developed from a lifetime of stage team driving. A yellow bandanna was tied tightly round one of his biceps in a crude attempt to staunch the flow of blood from a flesh wound.

Doc Jeffries had just finished wrapping a bandage round Tilson's head. 'This sure is one hell of a busy day,' he muttered as he snapped his bag shut. He followed Brad across the plaza to where the stage was standing.

'What happened, Hank?' Tilson asked as Doc Jeffries climbed up to inspect the guard who was slumped in an unnatural attitude.

'Four guys jumped us half an hour ago near Clear Water Creek,' the driver said hoarsely. 'They were waiting fer us. We never had a chance.' He glanced at the inert body beside him. 'They shot Al...'

'Right through the heart. There's nothing I can do fer him, I guess,' Doc Jeffries said laconically. He jumped down from the platform. 'You'd better send fer the mortician.'

'An' they robbed the lady,' the driver said hoarsely.

'Marie Madelaine!'

There was a horrified gasp from the onlookers as Brad stepped forward and opened the door. As he did so he found himself looking into the face portrayed on Johnson's photograph. With an effort, he kept his expression immobile as he held out his arm to assist Marie Madelaine to dismount from the coach. As he did so, he realised his gut reaction to the picture Johnson had so recently shown him was entirely vindicated – this woman was possessed with an overpowering personal magnetism.

'Marie, my dear! Are you sure you're not hurt?'

It was Joel Clayton who shouldered Brad aside and took hold of the woman's arm in a possessive manner.

There were no other passengers on the Concord. It was strange, but although Brad watched closely, Marie Madelaine showed no sign of concern over what had just happened. Indeed, as she dismounted, she seemed in a state of commendable composure compared to the jumpiness shown by the driver.

'In twenty years of drivin', I never see'd the like of it before.' The driver, his face smeared with dust, was holding forth to the crowd. 'I'm almost within sight of the town when these four guys appear. Before we know what's happening, one slug kills Al and another hits me. I try an' make a run fer it, but my arm goes numb an' it makes me lose control of the team an' the gang bring the horses to a stop. There ain't nuthin' more I could do.'

'Nobody's blamin' you fer anything,' Brad said. 'Did you recognise any of these guys?'

The man's eyes popped when he saw Brad's badge.

'No, sirree!' he exclaimed. 'They wore their bandannas on the lower halves of their faces and their hats were pulled low over their eyes. But they were Mexicans – that's fer sure. I could tell by their finery – an' they were talkin' Spanish.'

'Did they have a leader?'

'A leader? Well there was one guy who seemed a cut above the others. A caballero I reckon. He was dishin' out the orders. He was dressed the same way but he had a fist full of gold rings.'

'Some of General Diaz' men, maybe?' Tilson suggested.

'*Ladrones* more likely!' Victoria exclaimed contemptuously.

'Ain't no difference,' the driver remarked. 'They say Diaz is recruitin' anyone who'll ride with him.'

'No doubt they are now on their way back across the river,' Victoria said.

Brad grimaced. If she was right, once across the Rio Grande they would be secure in the infamous *Zona Libre*, a no-man's land that belonged to every bandit and outlaw between Mexico and the United States. No law held sway there and everyone could do as he wished – and usually did.

The driver slumped against the side of the coach as reaction set in. Sweat streamed down his dust-smeared face, his breath coming in even shorter gasps than that of the blown horses.

'Jesus, I surely need a drink,' he croaked.

'Take it easy, now,' Doc Jeffries said. 'I'll take a look at your arm.'

'What did they take?' Brad asked the driver as Doc Jeffries produced a bottle of iodine.

The driver backed away, his attention

45

distracted, his eyes apprehensive as Doc Jeffries seized his arm.

'Please, *monsieur*, let me finish the story for you.'

It was the woman who spoke. If all the male onlookers were not already looking at her, they did so now. Marie Madelaine faced her audience with the assurance of one used to being the centre of attention. 'These men, they stop the stage, they threaten to kill me if I do not give them my bag. What can I do?' Her speech carried a very strong French accent.

The circle of onlookers drew, back, the menfolk expressing a mixture of horror and regret. Even the women were sympathetic.

Marie dabbed a tear from the corner of her right eye with an embroidered silk handkerchief. It was a typical theatrical gesture, but to her admiring audience, it was the spectacle of a fragile woman, sorely tried and exerting massive self control over her emotions. It certainly made them lose control over theirs. A groundswell of emotion rose and united with the swelling tide of sympathy.

'Goldarn it! C'mon boys, what are we waiting for?' a hulking teamster roared. 'C'mon! Let's git after them!'

'Hold it!'

46

The plaza fell silent as Tilson bawled out with the voice of a stentor.

'No one's goin' anywhere until you're properly formed into a posse comitatus.'

The crowd murmured amongst themselves. 'Posse' they understood, but what the hell did 'comitatus' mean?

'Quit the fancy legal talk, McCracken, you're supposed to be Sheriff of Queensville,' Jake Rauchtenbauer said with a sneer. 'Just get after 'em.'

Tilson ignored him. 'Any man who wants to go after those *ladrones*, meets me outside my office in five minutes and gets himself properly sworn in, otherwise they don't ride.'

As the men in the crowd rushed to fetch their horses, Tilson turned to Brad.

'You comin'?'

Brad shook his head. 'I guess I'll stay right here and make a few enquiries.'

'Suit yourself.'

As Tilson turned to go, Brad caught his arm. Sensing the youngster's disappointment, he said, 'I guess this is your first posse?'

Tilson nodded.

'I gotta warn you. Come dusk, these brave citizens of yours will soon lose their enthusiasm.'

'Dusk? We should have caught them long

47

before then.'

'I wouldn't count on it. They got an hour's start.'

'So, we'll make camp overnight and follow 'em next morning.'

'Across the Rio Grande? This posse of yours will have seen the light long before then. Only fools and outlaws go into the *Zona Libre*. Lawmen keep clear.'

'You reckon they'll desert me?'

'Sure they will. I've seen it happen many times before. An' when it happens, do me a favour, will you? Don't risk your neck chasin' after those guys on your own. I reckon they're the same bunch that tried to ride us down just now.'

Tilson's eyes widened. 'All the more reason to get after 'em, then.'

'But not on your own,' Brad insisted.

Tilson looked puzzled. 'Why not? In any case, once these men are sworn in they'll have to obey my orders.'

Brad looked at him cynically. 'Now see here, Tilson. I figure your place is right here in Queensville, not chasin' your ass off over half the county.'

'You're just like everyone else,' Tilson said sullenly. 'You think I'm too young and inexperienced for this job. Or maybe a stage being held up and robbed ain't important enough to you.'

'That's as may be,' Brad agreed. 'Everyone has to make a start. Either you profit from the advice of others – or learn the hard way. Think about it. There's no way you're gonna catch up with those *ladrones*. If they are Diaz' men, there's no way they're gonna ride directly back to his camp. Once they get across the Rio Grande and into the *Zona Libre* that's the last you're gonna see of 'em.'

'What do you suggest I do? If I stay here and do nothin' folks'll think I ain't even tryin'.'

'If I were you, I'd quit worryin' about what people think. You'll never please everybody, that's fer sure. Sweep your own backyard first. You can move further out once you've earned a reputation. In the law game you seldom get a second chance. Remember, big as you are, one bullet is all it takes to kill you.'

As Tilson walked away, Brad turned to Marie who was standing with Clayton in front of the hotel. Again it registered with Brad that for a woman who had just been robbed, she was remarkably collected; but the twitch in one of Clayton's facial muscles indicated he was edgy as a steer on a thun-

49

dery night. Just what was on this man's mind?

'I'll just go check with the desk and see if they have your room ready, Marie,' Clayton muttered, as though anxious to get away.

'But, *monsieur le ranger*, why are you not riding with the posse?' Marie Madelaine asked Brad. Her eyes widened as she spoke and Brad was made vividly aware of the casual way she expected to dominate him by her unique physical attraction.

He met her gaze coolly. 'Why, Miss Madelaine, a stage coach bein' robbed is a common enough occurrence in these parts. If I investigated every crime I came across I'd surely be chasin' my tail.'

'You must have many interesting stories to tell, *monsieur*, maybe we should talk about them, sometime?'

'I'd like that, Miss Madelaine.'

'Oh call me Marie, please. Everyone does.'

'Ranger Saunders, may I speak with you for a moment?'

Victoria Clayton approached them, her arms full of schoolbooks. As she drew nearer, Brad became aware of her antipathy to Marie. Nothing was said, it was the way she looked at her ... and then cut her dead. But if she was nonplussed at the other woman's attitude towards her, Marie didn't show it.

Clayton appeared in the doorway of the hotel. 'Everything's OK, Marie, your room is ready for you,' he said.

'If you will excuse me, *monsieur*, I must change,' Marie said to Brad.

Clayton hastened to open the door for her and followed her inside.

Victoria Clayton turned and set off across the street and entered the plaza. Brad caught up with her in a few strides.

'Miss Victoria, mind if I walk with you a-ways?'

The girl's frosty expression melted. For the first time Brad realised she was a very good-looking young woman, despite the severity of her schoolma'am appearance.

'I guess not,' she said, patting her blonde curls into place underneath her bonnet.

'How come you dislike Marie Madelaine so much?'

The girl grimaced. 'Woman's intuition, I guess. There's somethin' false about her.'

'Like what?' Brad persisted.

Victoria smiled back at him with her mouth, but not with her eyes. One of the books she was holding, Webster's Blue-Back Speller, fell to the ground and Brad retrieved it for her.

'Pa's bin actin' plain stupid 'bout her ever since he met her on a business trip to New Orleans. He even went to San Antonio just to hear her sing. He's been moonin' over her ever since.'

'Ain't you bein' a mite unkind, Miss Victoria?'

'Well, I guess I don't like him fallin' fer someone he knows nothin' about. Ma's only been dead these twelve months. Ain't no cause for him to charge about like a deranged steer.'

Their walk had taken them across the plaza to the entry of a tree-lined road along which were several private houses with gardens overlooking the sea. Brad only saw the sea now and again and it fascinated him. As he gazed across the bay, the sight of a ship in full sail gave him a nostalgic boyhood re-minder of a lone covered wagon rolling across the wide windswept country of the Panhandle.

They paused to watch Tilson lead the posse out of the plaza but his horse was skittish and as he rode past, he did not notice them.

Victoria stopped by the gate of one of the houses. It was a large adobe structure built in hacienda style with a shady stoop overlooking a spacious garden full of flowers which a coloured gardener was watering using a bucket and a small stirrup pump. He was being supervised by a grey haired middle-aged woman wearing a calico dress. The woman acknowledged Victoria with a wave of her hand.

'The ranch is four hours outa town so I live here with my Aunt Maud during term time,' Victoria explained. 'It's nice and handy for the school. Tilson's mother lives here, right next door, so I guess I'll stop by and tell her he's away on a wild goose chase.'

'What makes you say that?' Brad picked her up immediately.

The girl gave a wry smile. 'I ain't never seen a posse leave Queensville yet that didn't eat dust before it came back from the banks of the Rio Grande empty-handed and spittin' feathers. It's their way of lettin' off steam – just like one of those locomotives they're always saying they're gonna put through Queensville into Mexico one day. Chance'll be a fine thing – it'll take a revolution to make Lerdo's government change its mind. But whether General Diaz and his rag-tag of an army can do it is a matter for debate. I don't know what you think but I don't hold with our government allowing him here in south west Texas, we're gettin' too many

53

Mexes running around thinkin' they own the place.'

Brad admired the girl's shrewd observation. She was a born Texan. He said, 'I gather you don't like Tilson being a lawman?'

The girl flushed.

'Tilson's got brains. His uncle was a wealthy rancher in Montana. When he died, he left Tilson a legacy to pay for his legal studies in San Francisco. But when his father was killed he lost interest in his studies and despite all the persuading his ma and I gave him, he wouldn't go back after the funeral. I believe he's livin' in hope of catchin' up with his father's killer. Fat chance, when you rangers couldn't come up with the killer. I warned him he's wastin' his time, but he just won't listen. Can't you guys catch whoever's responsible?'

'I guess we're still workin' on it,' Brad told her, trying not to sound lame.

'Well, after Tilson gave up his law studies he persuaded the townsfolk to elect him sheriff. His mother and I begged him not to put up for it.' Victoria pulled a wry face. 'But I guess Tilson got the job on a sympathy vote. What a waste!'

'Seems like he can look after himself,' Brad observed gently.

The girl smiled scornfully. 'You reckon?' Her cool appraisal almost unnerved Brad. 'Mister, you're a ranger – an' it shows. You don't wear fancy clothes and strut around like a peacock. You walk around kinda watchful – like a guy who's got eyes in the back of his head. You know what you're about – word is you had your gun out and were firing before you hit the dirt when those guys attacked you in the plaza. How come it was Tilson who got shot rather than you?'

Brad winced. This young woman was as straight as four aces. Tilson was a lucky guy to have her rooting for him.

'Maybe you gotta let him have his head a bit,' he suggested lamely.

Victoria passed through the gate and closed it. She pointed to the schoolhouse.

'Listen,' she said scornfully. 'Tilson's got more to offer than be a common lawman.' She caught Brad's eye and flushed deep red. 'Gee, I'm sorry, Ranger Saunders. I guess I didn't mean that. It's my big mouth again.'

'Never apologise when you're right,' Brad said with a bleak smile. He recalled his earlier conversation with Tilson about Rauchtenbauer. 'Tell me about Jake Rauchtenbauer, is he sweet on you, too?'

Victoria looked stunned. For a moment

Brad thought he had overstepped the mark and winced at the expectation of a slap across the face.

Her expression changed to wonderment. 'Why, you ain't been in town five minutes and you've gotten us all figured out!' she exclaimed.

'It's my job,' Brad observed dryly.

'Well, Jake Rauchtenbauer owns the Black Joke Saloon. He's been successful in business and he seemed to figure that gave him the right to come callin' on me.'

'You do anythin' to encourage that?' Brad asked.

Victoria flushed pink to the lobes of her ears. 'After Tilson and I fell out over this sheriff business I went to a barn dance with Jake. I guess maybe I figured on teaching Tilson a lesson.'

'Playin' with fire?'

Victoria nodded. 'Somethin' like that. But we teachers are only human after all.'

'I guess you got your sums wrong,' Brad commented dryly.

Victoria nodded miserably. She shuddered. 'I don't trust Jake Rauchtenbauer. He dresses fancy and talks smooth but he ain't fer me. There's somethin' about him that gives me the creeps. When Tilson found out I'd been out with him, he was kinda … upset. Now he and Jake are bristlin' like two dogs for a fight.'

She gripped Brad's arm. 'But do you see what I mean?' she whispered, her voice choking as she spoke. 'I'll level with you, Ranger Saunders. I'm in love with Tilson. The plan was we'd marry when he qualified. I don't wanna see him get backshot by some outlaw in a dark alley. He's got more to offer than be a soft touch for some gunslinger that ain't fit to clean his boots.'

Across the way the church bell began to toll.

The door of the house opened and a handsome, silver haired woman appeared. Her careworn face was as pale as porcelain and she was dressed entirely in black and holding a bible and a rosary. She smiled wanly when she saw Victoria.

'That's Tilson's mother,' Victoria whispered. 'She's goin' to church right now, so I'll speak with her afterwards. She ain't never been the same since her husband was murdered. She was never happy about him being sheriff. If anything happens to Tilson, it would destroy her completely. Everyday she goes to church and prays he'll give up this crazy idea of being a lawman.' She gripped Brad's arm so fiercely it made him wince. 'Ranger Saunders, you've gotta help me to get him to see reason – please!'

FOUR

Clayton followed Marie Madelaine like a faithful dog along the corridor to her room. He waited by the door while the chamber maid left before whispering anxiously, 'Marie, I gotta know – is the deal still on? Only I've a meetin' with Valdez over at the hotel at eight o'clock.'

Marie walked over to the gilt framed mirror to pat her ash blonde chignon into place.

'Do not worry, *cheri,*' she said, smiling at Clayton through the mirror. 'The money is quite safe. Tomorrow you will be able to collect your cattle.'

The relief on Clayton's face was palpable. His expression relaxed.

'Cattle!' he exclaimed, 'they ain't just *cattle!* Why, Marie, we're talkin' about a hundred head of the best Mexican bloodstock. With an investment like this, your brother and I are gonna be the biggest cattle barons in the south west.'

'You are forgetting, *cheri*, my brother is already a marquis,' Marie said with a low laugh.

Clayton's expression turned to puzzlement. 'But those Mexican road agents stole your bag ... how come you still have the money?'

Marie patted his arm. 'Do not concern yourself, *cheri*. The money wasn't in the bag.'

Clayton stared at her. 'Why, Marie, where on earth have you hidden it?'

Marie came closer and patted his cheek. The aroma of her French perfume was an intoxicating pot-pourri of flowers and musk.

'Marie, you know I'm wild about you...' Clayton muttered hoarsely as he slipped his arms about her, but she pushed him gently away.

'I told you, do not concern yourself about the money,' Marie said. 'I have a much more serious problem, *cheri.*' Her lips pouted and her forehead puckered into a frown as she spoke.

Instantly Clayton became the epitome of middle-aged solicitude. 'Marie, if there's anythin' I can do...'

'My bag was taken. All my dresses have gone. I have nothing to wear when I sing tonight.'

Clayton stroked his jaw in rapt contemplation of this unusual problem. Border towns like Queensville did not boast shops which specialised in haute couture.

Marie gave a twirl. 'How can I appear before my audience like this?'

Clayton snapped his fingers. 'Wait a minute,' he exclaimed. 'You an' Victoria are both about the same size. Maybe she can lend you a dress.'

Marie burst out laughing. 'Oh Joel, *cheri* you are priceless! Do you think your daughter likes me enough to lend me one of her dowdy little dresses?'

'Now wait a minute, my Victoria's dresses ain't dowdy!' Clayton exploded.

Marie laughed at his discomfiture.

'One moment, *cheri!*' she exclaimed. 'And all will be revealed.'

She disappeared into the dressing room. Clayton lit a cigar and spent the next few minutes pacing the room. This woman was like no other he had ever met. He had been under her spell ever since the day he had heard her sing in the salon of a Mississippi steamboat whilst on an abortive business trip to New Orleans with the object of raising a loan from a so-called friend who was president of a bank.

Angry and disappointed at the curt refusal, he had fallen in with the Marquis de Bau and his dazzlingly attractive sister. The resulting conversation was engraved permanently in his mind. The marquis had talked about the cattle industry knowledgeably and expressed sympathy with Clayton's desire for an injection of capital into the Lazy Z.

'I understand that a certain General Porfirio Diaz is planning a revolution south of the border,' the marquis said, smoothly. 'An idea which I believe finds favour with the United States Government?'

'Lerdo's Government is opposed to lettin' the railroad companies into Mexico,' Clayton replied. 'Our Government have turned a blind eye to Diaz raising an army this side of the Rio Grande.'

The marquis nodded. 'The Mexican Government have put one of their agents into Diaz' camp. A man called Colonel Carlos Valdez. He is known to you, I believe?'

'Colonel Valdez? Sure I know him. He's in charge of the commissariat. I've negotiated a coupla beef contracts with him to supply Diaz' men. But I had no idea he was working for the Mexican Government. What's his game?'

The marquis leaned forward confiden-tially. 'How would you like a chance to make just a little more than a few hundred dollars from a beef contract?'

'What are you sayin'?'

'The Mexican Government have asked me to supply them with a hundred thousand dollars...'

'A hundred thousand!'

'...in counterfeit money.'

'Counterfeit money? What the hell do they want with that?'

'The plan is that Valdez will tell General Diaz it is aid from the US Government.'

'But if contractors like me got paid in counterfeit money, the Treasury agents will come sniffin' round. When they trace it back to Diaz, his name will be mud.'

'Exactly.' The marquis sat back with a smile.

'So where do I fit into this deal?'

'The Mexican Government are offering to pay for this money with a herd of one hundred of their finest bloodstock bulls.'

Clayton whistled. He looked at the marquis in undisguised admiration. 'They must be worth all of ten grand.'

The marquis took a sip of Napoleon brandy and regarded Clayton with a scrutiny as keen as a falcon's.

'So, *mon ami* the herd is yours in return for a stake in your ranch. Once the money is passed to Valdez, there is no further risk to you.'

As Clayton pondered, the marquis continued, 'I think that this is an offer you cannot afford to refuse.'

Clayton came to his decision. 'OK, you're on.' He held out his hand as he spoke.

The marquis smiled. 'Together you and I shall own the biggest ranch in the south west...'

There was a rustle and as Clayton looked up, he gasped.

As to a cue, Marie appeared, bringing him back to the present. She was wearing a red dress cut so low it seemed that any moment her breasts would explode out of the decolletage. Black sleeve-length gloves completed an outfit which left him dry-mouthed and speechless.

'What is the matter, *cheri*? You do not like it?' A pair of diamond studded pendant earrings framed her face as she smiled bewitchingly at him.

Clayton nodded, dry-mouthed. 'But, Marie, you said those guys had taken your bag?'

Marie's teeth, perfectly formed, gleamed

as her lips curved in an ingenuous smile. 'You do not think I would allow them to steal anything of value? I was wearing this underneath my travelling dress.'

As Brad re-entered the main street, a freckle-faced youngster came loping towards him.

'Hey, mister ranger!' he yelled. 'Come quickly! Ole Dan Jasper's bin murdered!'

Brad's face hardened. 'Take it easy, son,' he told the little boy. 'Just take me along a-ways.'

Brad followed the youngster until they came to a little knot of people gathered in front of the barber shop. As Brad approached it, he felt his spirits lower.

'Say, what's this place comin' to? Ole Dan Jasper never did anyone any harm,' the owner of the restaurant next door remarked in a loud voice meant for Brad to hear.

'OK – now everyone just go about your business and leave this to me,' Brad said as he shouldered his way through the gathering crowd.

He entered the shop, walked past the shiny leather chair which had seen Dan Jasper's last customer and paused at the foot of the stairs. Catching sight of his stubble-darkened face in the mirror reminded Brad of his own need of a shave. As he mounted the stairs he became aware of the sound of a woman sobbing.

From the doorway he saw a middle-aged woman standing beside a young man, about ten years his junior, who had his arms around her. The unlit cigar stuck between his lips was chewed to shreds.

'I'm Pete Jasper,' the young man said when he saw Brad. 'This here's my ma.'

Keeping a tight rein on his emotions, Brad walked over to the bed and drew back the blanket. As he bent over his third corpse of the day, he saw the proud flesh round the tight bonds securing the hands and feet and the bandanna drawn equally tightly over the nose and mouth leaving the purple bloated visage of the suffocated man half-exposed to view.

Brad had seen many images of death, but this one revolted him. A cold anger welled up inside him as he swore softly under his breath. What kind of man was this who could stoop to such cruelty?

'I met Dan during the war,' Brad said. 'He did a real close shave in camp when he wasn't ridin' with Jeb Stuart.'

'You knew him?' Pete said.

Brad nodded. 'He was a real nice guy. One

of the best.'

'I don't understand it. No money's gone. They ain't stolen a thing,' Pete Jasper said in a voice choking with emotion. 'Pa had a weak heart. He was never the same after he was taken prisoner. Why in God's name did they have to rope him up as tight as that?'

'I would never have known had I not come by and seen the place closed,' Mrs Jasper said. 'Dan never closed early in his life.'

Brad grimaced as he drew away from the corpse, sympathy for the distraught woman and her son mingling with the coldness of his anger at the man who must have calmly watched Dan Jasper die. He laid both hands on Mrs Jasper's shoulders and kissed her forehead gently.

With an effort he forced himself to cast a professional eye over the scene. Two discarded cigar butts had left slight burns on the floorboards where they had been recently ground out. As he walked over to the open window, his searching glance noticed a spent shell case and an empty bottle of tequila lying beside it. He sniffed slightly, almost fancying he could smell a whiff of gunsmoke lingering in the foetid atmosphere.

When he drew back the curtain and looked across the street at the Grand Palace

Hotel, he knew he had come to the exact spot where the killer of Eli Johnson had hidden.

Brad rasped the stubble on his chin thoughtfully. It was plain that the killer had known exactly which hotel room Johnson had taken. He had figured out precisely where to come to shoot him. And in his desire to carry out his objective he had subjected Dan Jasper to a slow, agonising death with two objectives in view; one, to eliminate him as a witness, and two, to avoid the sound of a death cry.

The measured tread of boots on the staircase foretold the arrival of the mortician and his assistants.

'Sorry we took so long,' the mortician said morosely. He was a tall thin man dressed in a black suit. A cigarette dangled out of the corner of his mouth. He regarded the corpse with professional detachment.

'The cause of death was by asphyxiation. You'll need the coroner to confirm that,' Brad told him.

The mortician gave a sepulchral cough and nodded agreement. 'What with one thing and another, we bin rushed off our feet today,' he said with a sigh.

'Well, what are you gonna do about it?'

Pete Jasper demanded harshly of Brad as they watched the mortician's assistants set about the task of removing the corpse.

Brad bit his lip. Pete Jasper's bitter anger and deep-seated frustration was something he shared. Men like Eli Johnson took a calculated risk when they entered the law game; Brad himself was keenly aware that death lurked round every corner when you chose to deal with the dregs of society. But Dan Jasper had been going about his lawful business until only a few hours ago and had lost his life simply because it suited someone to take it.

'Pete, you look after your ma. I'll take care of this,' Brad said softly.

But Brad was by no means as certain of himself as his manner implied. What he needed was some clue, however small which might lead him to the identity of Dan Jasper's killer.

When he reached the bottom of the stairs, he paused as he caught sight of the orderly row of shaving mugs hanging from their hooks, each inscribed with the name of Dan Jasper's regular customers.

One mug was missing.

A glance revealed it was standing on the counter in front of the chair with a brush, a used towel and a pair of scissors.

Curiosity made Brad step forward and pick up the mug. It hadn't been washed, for traces of shaving foam still lingered round the rim. Brad turned the cup to view the side and saw no name, but the initials: *JR*.

Judging by the others it must be a name too long to paint on a shaving mug...

Jake Rauchtenbauer!

Renata Orsini urged the little pinto to the top of the ridge until she reined in alongside her father. Dribbles of fresh blood shone wet on the dun-coloured fur of two rabbits tied to the saddle of her horse; food for the pot, they had been shot with the Winchester rifle she wore slung in a bandolier across her back. Seagulls soared overhead in a sky of washed-out blue and, looking behind her, over the miles of broken patches of mesquite bush she could just see the sun glinting silver off the wavecaps of the Gulf of Mexico.

Franco Orsini scratched his Roman nose thoughtfully.

'I think that maybe we should go home now,' he said. Although he had emigrated to the States from Italy twenty years ago, he still retained traces of his native Lombardy accent.

'It's getting late, papa,' Renata said. Wearing levis, the only concession to her sex was the slight thrust of her firm young breasts against her check shirt. She adjusted her sombrero as she spoke.

Franco leaned forward on the pommel of his horse and looked fondly at the only daughter to his Irish wife. Renata was doing her best to be the son he had never had. But it wasn't a woman's job to ride and shoot and herd cattle. Renata was eighteen now, time for a young woman to marry and start a family of her own. Even if he took the biased view of a father, with his hand on his heart he could not say his daughter was beautiful. He shrugged philosophically. Four years of bitter fighting with the 5th Louisiana Infantry during the war had, done nothing to shake his unwavering faith in the Catholic religion. What could a man do when Almighty God decreed that a man have nothing else from his marriage but one daughter who was a tomboy?

He cast about him. In the mesquite, over to his right a couple of mavericks whisked their tails and eyed him balefully. Franco had emigrated from Italy to better himself but since the war had ended life in his adopted country had been harder than ever. Working in the mass-production factories in the east might have paid better, but after service in the Confederate army, the confinement of such a life did not appeal to him. Even so, it was all he could do to try to build a small herd and scrape a living from this land...

'Look, papa, there are men coming this way!'

Franco peered in the direction his daughter was pointing. The sun was at his back so he had no difficulty in picking up the plume of dust spotted by his keen-eyed daughter.

'Why do they ride so fast, papa?'

Renata kneed her horse forward as she spoke.

'Wait!'

She obeyed as her father came alongside her.

'I think maybe they hurry to get away from someone,' he said.

'Are they outlaws?'

Renata unslung her rifle. She had large, capable hands which checked the loading of her weapon with the dexterity of a trained infantryman. Franco had taught her well.

'Look, they are coming this way!' she exclaimed.

She raised the Winchester.

'Wait!' Franco leaned across and palmed the barrel down. 'They are four. Do you want to bring them about us like hornets? Follow me.'

The girl followed her father obediently as he dropped below the low ridge. With a soldier's eye for cover he used the dead ground it provided to follow a course which would bring them closer to the men without being seen.

Five minutes later, Renata leaned across and tugged her father's sleeve.

'Voices. Speaking in Spanish,' she whispered.

Franco nodded. *'Ladrones!'* he exclaimed contemptuously. 'Probably with Diaz' rabble of an army. They have been up to no good, I believe.'

He unsheathed his rifle, dismounted and dropping on his belly crawled crabwise through the low scrub until he reached the top of the ridge. After a brief glance over the top, he signalled for Renata to join him. She drew her own weapon and following his example, after a few moments appeared alongside him.

Her father held his finger to his lips and pointed. Renata eased forward on her lean belly until she could see over the ridge below. 'Keep still until they gone,' Franco whispered. 'If we draw their attention they will attack us. It is not our business they are discussing. We must not interfere.'

Colonel Carlos Valdez reined in and waited for his *compadres* to join him.

Garcia arrived first, his face fixed in the permanently mocking smile that character-ised its usual expression. The other two riders, Pedro, a wiry little man with a face like squeezed orange and the grossly fat Manuel followed him.

'I do not think the gringos are following us!' Valdez exclaimed triumphantly as the others gathered round him. 'So, I think now we will see how rich we have become.'

They dismounted. Garcia and the other two waited impatiently while Valdez un-strapped a large portmanteau from his horse. When he found it was locked, Valdez drew his revolver and the shot which blew open the lock raised a covey of partridges clattering out of the brush.

He dipped his hand inside the portmanteau and withdrew an intimate item of ladies underwear. Raucous shouts of laughter filled the air as Manuel cavorted around pretend-ing to wear it. A silk dress followed. After similar treatment it was cast carelessly to one side and trampled on as the men gathered closely round the rapidly emptying portmanteau. A scent spray received a similar fate after the contents had been doused liberally over the protagonists with hoots of infantile laughter.

Suddenly the group fell silent. The expression on Valdez' face turned to anger and disgust as his fingers clawed at the bottom of the portmanteau. He turned it over and jumped on it to check that there was no false bottom to it.

'You told us the woman was carrying a hundred thousand dollars,' Garcia said softly. 'A gift from the American government to General Diaz.'

As he spoke, his right hand moved surreptitiously towards one of the knives strapped to his hips.

Valdez swore softly under his breath.

'Look, we are being followed!' Pedro pointed to a cloud of dust on the horizon as he spoke.

Garcia led Manuel and Pedro in the scramble for the horses, but Valdez ignored their mad dash for safety and remained behind. Working quickly, he gathered the loose items of clothing together in a pile, took out a box of lucifers and struck one...

When Franco saw Valdez strike a lucifer and set fire to the woman's clothing, a great rage surged within him. He knew he must act quickly or the fire would ignite the tinder dry mesquite brush and spread all over the range unhindered for mile after mile, driving the handful of mavericks which remained away forever. They were the only source of his slender livelihood and for that he was prepared to fight as hard as he had ever done in the war. With the *ladrones* disappearing in a cloud of dust in the direction of the Rio Grande, he felt able to intervene at last.

'Be careful, papa!' Renata cried.

But Franco was beyond all reason. Renata was strong, but she could not hold him. He snatched up his rifle, leapt to his feet and with a loud rebel yell, charged down the slope towards the startled Mexican.

Renata rose to her feet and raised her rifle, unable to fire for fear of hitting her father. She watched helplessly as the two men clashed head on.

'Papa!' she cried as a shot rang out and Franco keeled over, dropping his rifle with a metallic clatter on the rocks as he fell.

Renata's anguished cry drew the attention of Valdez. Dropping to one knee, she felt the bullet from his gun fan her cheek. Renata was a good shot. The two rabbits tied in her saddle hung in mute testimony to that. She went down on one knee, as her father had taught her and sighted her rifle on the fleeing Mexican. But shooting animals for the pot is one thing, shooting a fellow human being is, another and like many an infantryman before her, she fell victim to self-doubt. As a result, her trembling hands aimed her own shot wide.

She watched in disbelief as Valdez leapt into his saddle at a run and spurred his horse savagely into headlong flight into the trackless waste of mesquite brush.

Renata stood up and systematically emptied the magazine of her Winchester after the retreating figure, but the fire had caught hold, raising clouds of smoke which obscured her aim.

She cast her weapon aside in her haste to reach her father. But even as she stumbled towards him, his clothing caught fire. She screamed in horror as the unthinkable happened. By now the heat from the flames was raging hot as from an oven and try as she may she could not get through to where her father lay. Mercifully, he was already dead, for there was no sign of movement as the flames consumed him.

Beaten back by the flames, Renata stood foursquare as she gazed impotently in the direction in which the Mexicans had fled.

'One day I shall find you. And then I shall kill you all!' she screamed.

And as the pall of smoke drifted, revealing the blood-red orb of the setting sun, the flames crackled and roared a fiery litany of death as they devoured the body of former Louisiana infantryman, Franco Orsini.

FIVE

Brad strode out of the late Dan Jasper's barber shop, his face set hard. It was time he made his presence felt in certain quarters.

'I guess Mr Rauchtenbauer is too busy to see anyone,' the shirt sleeved barkeep answered Brad's query with a gap-toothed smile and shrug of indifference as he polished a glass behind the bar of the Black Joke Saloon. His sentence was punctuated with the sustained rapping of a hammer as a carpenter put the finishing touches to a brand new stage. 'He's gettin' ready fer Miss Madelaine's show tonight.'

'I wasn't askin' a favour,' Brad snapped. 'I wanna see him, *pronto*. Where is he?'

'Who's askin'?'

Brad turned to see a couple of mestizos dressed in black suits. They had the well-muscled shoulders and slim hips of Spanish bred fighting bulls. It was plain they were employed for one purpose only – to protect the Black Joke Saloon from the depredations of drunkards.

As they closed in on him, Brad flipped back his vest and allowed their surprised eyes to dwell on his badge for all of two seconds. It occurred to Brad that they must be the only people in Queensville who didn't know who he was. Just in case they had second thoughts, his Colt appeared in his right hand with the rapidity of an eyeblink.

'Now, boys, you wouldn't wanna fall foul of the law, would you?' Brad said pointing to his silver star. 'If you don't wanna spend the next week coolin' off in jail, take me to Jake Rauchtenbauer.'

As he holstered his weapon with a twirl, the hired muscle moved, albeit with some reluctance. They sauntered through the handful of gawping early evening drinkers and honky tonks dressed in their frilly red and green outfits up the raked staircase which led down to the newly-constructed stage.

Gilt candelabra hung from the ceiling and a three-pronged version stood somewhat pretentiously on top of a piano at which an elderly man wearing a dark green eye shade, a cigarette dangling from his lips, was busy tuning. Tilson was right, the whole place was a cut above the average frontier saloon.

The hired muscle mounted the red-carpeted staircase, turned left along a corridor, walked to the far end and paused in front of a door on which was painted the legend, OFFICE.

'OK, now beat it,' Brad ordered.

He waited while the two muscleheads retreated, marvelling how it had taken two of them to do what one could have done. He knocked on the door and turned the handle. It was locked, so he knocked again, louder this time.

'Who is it?' Rauchtenbauer's voice said irritably.

Brad told him.

When the door opened and Jake Rauchtenbauer appeared the reason for the locked door became obvious. He was adjusting the velvet collar of his jacket which he had hastily put on. Behind him, one of his girls was adjusting her dress.

'How the hell did you get in here?' Rauchtenbauer demanded. 'I told the boys I was busy.'

'So it seems,' Brad agreed as the girl brushed past him with an overpowering smell of scent and a dazzling smile. 'I want it we should talk.'

Rauchtenbauer's ruggedly handsome features broke into an engaging grin.

'Why, Ranger Saunders, I'd be happy to oblige, but I got a business to attend to. Why, Miss Madelaine is due on stage in a couple of hours. She's mighty temperamental and if things ain't just right...'

'Seems like it wasn't botherin' you just now,' Brad said sarcastically.

For a moment there was a battle of wills until Rauchtenbauer thought the better of it and capitulated. He led the way back into his office. It was sumptuously furnished with a glass-topped oak desk and a swivel chair covered with black leather.

'Drink?' Rauchtenbauer's hands hovered over a bottle and glasses as he waited for an answer.

Brad shook his head. He found it hard to

conceal his dislike of men like Rauchtenbauer. They ran their affairs right on a knife-edge, always just contriving to keep the right side of the law. No wonder Ranger Miller had his suspicions. Where had he got his money from to pay for the Black Joke? He let the thought wander through his mind as he waited while the other man poured himself a stiff measure and downed half of it.

'Dan Jasper's been murdered,' Brad said in a matter-of-fact voice, all the while keenly observing Rauchtenbauer's reaction. But he seemed genuinely surprised at the news.

'Really? Well, now, Ranger Saunders, when did that happen?'

'Earlier today.' Brad deliberately kept his tone noncommittal.

'I guess I'm real upset about that. I wouldn't have figured a guy like Jasper had any enemies,' Rauchtenbauer said smoothly.

He's right, that was the irony of it Brad thought.

Rauchtenbauer lit a six-inch Havana. He inhaled deeply and blew out a cloud of smoke. 'You rangers have a reputation second to none. But I would have thought that Jasper's death was of no account to you. It's a routine matter for the sheriff. So, just

81

what brings you here, Ranger Saunders?'

'Any man's death means somethin' to me,' Brad told him. 'Young McCracken's still outa town. I thought to make a few enquiries on his behalf before the trail runs cold. Tell me, when did you last have a shave, Mr Rauchtenbauer?'

Brad slipped in the question as smoothly as a razor gliding through stubble. Visibly rattled, Rauchtenbauer's hand moved to smooth the cleanshaven lines of his jaw.

'Why I guess I stopped by Dan Jasper's place just before noon,' he replied.

'I take it you were alone there with him?'

Rauchtenbauer's eyes narrowed. 'There wasn't anyone else. Say, now wait a minute, you ain't trying to pin this one on me, are you?'

'Mister, we rangers don't go about pinning anythin' on anyone. We work strictly to the law. At this stage, all I do know is that you were Dan's last customer,' Brad said pointedly. 'There's your shavin' mug standing there to prove it.'

Rauchtenbauer leapt to his feet. 'Now hold it!' he protested. 'I wasn't Dan's last customer. There was another guy who came in just as Dan was cleaning me up. A Mexican who rides into town now and again. A guy named Valdez.'

'Colonel Valdez?'

Rauchtenbauer nodded. 'He's on General Diaz' staff.'

Brad pondered this piece of information. Back in San Antonio, McNelly had warned the Special Company that Diaz was planning a revolution. Brad's brow creased in puzzlement. Why should one of Diaz' henchmen want to shoot Johnson?

'How come you know this guy?' Brad demanded.

'He calls in here for a hand at cards when he rides into town to buy beef.'

'Who from?'

'Joel Clayton. He owns the Lazy Z Ranch.'

'Does this guy Valdez have any *compadres?*'

Rauchtenbauer nodded. 'Three, maybe four. One of 'em totes a pair of throwing knives. Name of Garcia.'

'That all you can tell me?'

Rauchtenbauer shrugged his broad shoulders. 'Just because a guy gambles a few dollars in my saloon don't mean to say I have to give him more than the time of day.'

Which just about summed Rauchtenbauer up as far as Brad was concerned.

'Whoa, fellas, there's smoke over yonder!'

Tilson exclaimed as he reined in his horse in a cloud of fine dust. The dozen possemen riding with him came to a halt beside him. After a couple of hours of hard riding, some of the more sedentary members of the posse were already showing signs of fatigue.

'They must have figured we weren't followin' and made camp fer the night,' one man observed.

'Yon's a mighty big camp fire,' another said laconically. 'I reckon a whole army could be sat round that.'

There was a murmur of agreement.

Suddenly they heard the sound of a rapid succession of shots.

'Come on, let's get over there,' Tilson snapped.

By the time they had covered the distance, the setting sun had been replaced by the great red glow of the fire which had by now spread over a square mile of country dense with tinder dry mesquite brush filling the air with the acrid tang of smoke.

'Some camp fire,' Tilson agreed as he drew so close his horse shied away from the heat of the flickering flames.

'There's no doin' nothin' 'bout this,' a posseman observed. 'I see'd fires like this afore. We ain't got no cause to do anythin 'bout it. The wind is fanning it towards the river, it ain't no threat to us in Queensville. It's gotta run its course. One thing fer sure, when it's through there ain't gonna be no trail left to foller in this burned out land, nohow.'

'He's right. Cain't see no future in this, Tilson,' another opined. 'I reckon we'd best head on back. There's a full moon tonight, iffen we make tracks rightaway, maybe we'll hit town afore midnight. I gotta thirst fit to drink the barrels dry.'

As the others murmured assent, Tilson rounded on them, his face full of scorn. Ranger Saunders had been right, these men were fickle, they'd ridden their tempers off and now all they wanted was to be home and in bed with their wives. Bearing in mind what Ranger Saunders had told him, he decided not to risk ordering them to remain for he would lose face if they ignored him.

'What you mean is you want to get back so's you can hear Marie Madelaine sing,' he said sarcastically.

'Anythin' wrong with that?' a man enquired. 'Why should we rough it out here, when there's creature comfort two hours' ride away?'

The others murmured assent.

'OK, do as you want, but I'm stayin' here-abouts,' he said contemptuously. 'I guess I'll make camp and take me a look around come first light.'

'Better watch out, Tilson boy, you might jest git yore arse burned,' one man said.

In an act of massive self control, Tilson ignored the bellow of laughter which followed. He was sick to death of these cheap jibes. He'd rather be on his own than beholden to anyone. He turned his horse away from the already retreating posse and began to follow a line away from the billowing clouds of smoke towards the direction of the shore.

After about a mile and a half of steady jogging he came to a long line of sand dunes following the line of the shore. Threading his way through the tall rank grass which grew here and there in a desultory fashion, he emerged onto the beach. He dismounted and leading his horse, he walked the short distance to the water's edge where the lines of breakers came rolling gently in. Behind him, the ghostly flicker of red light from the fire illuminated the horizon.

Suddenly he felt tired. It was so peaceful here. Out in the black void of the sea the lights of a distant vessel winked as he bent to dash some sea water to refresh his dust-smeared face.

Suddenly he became aware that he wasn't alone. Instinctively his hand forked for the Le Mat strapped to his hip, but his fingers were wet, they slipped awkwardly on the butt and he finished up highly conscious of the fact that he had bungled the draw.

'Take it easy, mister.'

Tilson lowered his weapon and stared in amazement at the shadowy figure standing in the moonlight. As his eyes narrowed into focus he saw what he thought was a young boy standing a few yards away from him.

'Who are you?' he demanded.

As he took a step forward, the figure backed away.

'Not so fast,' she said.

For a moment he thought he might be seeing an apparition, until he noticed the firm imprint of the girl's bare feet on the wet sand – and realised with a shock, that she was pointing a rifle at him.

'What are you doin' out here at this time of night?' he demanded.

The girl chuckled. 'There usually ain't nobody fer miles. Now who might you be?'

'Me? Why I'm Tilson McCracken. I'm a lawman.'

He tried to make it sound like an after-thought but his voice was bursting with pride as he spoke – even inside he felt a twinge of apprehension that should this girl choose to disbelieve him he might be teetering on the brink of death.

'I see your badge,' the girl replied as she drew closer. 'Mister, you're as jumpy as a grasshopper. Lucky fer you I ain't got an itchy trigger finger.'

She lowered the rifle and peered at him. Her eyes widening in a curiously innocent appraisal. 'My name's Renata. Say, Tilson, beggin' your pardon but you look mighty young to be totin' a law badge. What's your business out here?'

'I was leading a posse. We were chasin' after four guys who held up the Corpus stage an' shot the guard. I reckon they spotted us and fired the range. The rest of my men gave up when the fire came between us. They've no stomach for going on so they quit and headed back to Queensville. Say did you see anythin' of these guys?'

'Sure.' The girl shivered as she spoke. 'Look, it's gettin' cool out here. Bring your horse and I'll tell you 'bout it back at the house.'

Tilson did as she asked and led his horse

alongside her in silence as she led the way beyond the dunes for about a quarter of a mile until they came to a wooden framed cottage with a couple of outbuildings cunningly hidden until the last moment when they came into view. The building was quite safe from the fire, which was over a mile away, the flames being fanned by the stiffening breeze off the sea, carrying the inferno further inland towards the Rio Grande.

'Renata, is that you?' a woman's voice called anxiously as they entered the yard.

'That's ma,' the girl said. 'Set your horse in yonder barn, Tilson. There's feed an' water there. Come along in when you're ready. We've rabbit stew in the pot.'

Tilson did as he was bidden. When he was satisfied he had done all he could for the animal he closed up the barn and walked over to the house.

'To be sure and why in God's name were you talkin' with a strange man?' a woman's voice scolded in a broad Irish-American accent as he approached. 'Do you not have any shred of dignity left, child? Have we not troubles enough?'

'Aw shucks, ma. I ain't puny enough fer a feller to come sparkin' fer me an' you know it.'

The two women fell silent as Tilson pushed open the door, hinged with rawhide, and walked in.

'Now off you be going to bed. Quickly now, will ye move!'

In the dim light of an oil lamp, Tilson became aware of the bulky figure of the woman ushering her daughter away, but the girl ignored her mother's chiding and held her ground.

'Ma, I just told you, this man is the Sheriff of Queensville.'

The woman peered at Tilson through the gloom. Her eyes were red as though she had been weeping, yet it had done nothing to diminish the power of her personality. This was a woman from whom crying did not come easily...

'Why, you must be Abe McCracken's boy!' she exclaimed. 'I heard you'd been elected sheriff. We heard your father had been murdered...'

Tilson flinched as the woman's tough exterior cracked and she broke down in tears. As he felt the hurt of her reminder piling up inside him, it took him all his self-control to bring his own emotion under control. Suddenly it dawned on him that there was far more to administering the law than he'd ever realised.

'I guess there's somethin' you oughta know,' Renata said, turning to face Tilson.

Tilson felt his blood run cold as he listened to the girl's account of what had happened on the mesquite range. As she finished the first tear ran down her cheek, the first indication of her massive self-control breaking down.

God Almighty what manner of men are these? thought Tilson.

He stepped forward, trying to control his own distress, and in an act of common humanity he took the girl in an embrace. Her bosom heaved in a great choking sob as all her pent-up emotion gushed forth with all the force of a wave pounding onto the nearby shore.

Suddenly she tore herself away from him and ran into another room, slamming the door behind her. All the while Renata's mother had been standing in silence silhouetted in the eerie yellow glow of the lamp. When Renata had gone she pointed a bony finger at Tilson.

'So you are a lawman? Then act like one! How can decent God-fearing people survive in this wilderness without the protection of the law? I want justice!' Her voice rose to a screech of fear mingled with bitter anger. 'D'you hear me? I want justice for the death of my man!'

In the wild mesquite brakes just short of the Rio Grande, Colonel Valdez brought his mount to a stop. As he cast backwards over the smoke-blackened sky, there was no sign of pursuit.

'So, we return to General Diaz empty-handed.' Garcia spoke softly, but his hooded eyes were full of menace and his hand strayed dangerously near the hilt of one of his knives. 'So much for your plan to make us rich.'

Even as Garcia's hand moved, Valdez drew his Colt. 'Do not think of it, my friend,' he said softly. He waited while Garcia relaxed. 'We have not finished yet,' he continued, holstering his weapon as though nothing had happened. He smiled as he spoke. The danger was over for the moment now he had established his superiority. As Garcia's ugly mood subsided, Valdez gave full rein to the glib tongue which had talked him out of many a scrape in the past.

'The woman still has the money, of that I am sure,' he told them.

'Then how do you suggest we get it, senor?' Garcia asked ingenuously.

Valdez pondered this vital question.

He consulted his gold pocket watch. Eight o'clock. It was impossible for him to return to Queensville in time for what would, if Johnson hadn't turned up, have been a profitable meeting with Joel Clayton.

He shook his head in disbelief. Human gullibility knew no bounds. For that fool of a Frenchman to believe that there would be a herd of bloodstock bulls waiting to be exchanged for a hundred thousand pounds of his counterfeit money staggered him. That was the tempting prospect he, as Lerdo's agent, had held out to the marquis at their secret meeting in New Orleans.

But Johnson's arrival had ruined his plans. The coded telegraph message warning him of the American agent's imminent appearance in Queensville had nearly arrived too late. With Johnson and the rangers on the trail, the whole deal would have had to be called off. And that would have meant the sacrifice of one hundred thousand dollars. A fact which grieved him greatly, for Valdez' plan was not only to follow his government's orders to dupe the marquis, but also for him to dupe them by grabbing it for himself. A double-cross within a double-cross. The idea was at once neat, appealing and profitable.

Valdez had spent his whole life working at the behest of his parsimonious masters; with their overthrow in sight, he wasn't prepared to let this chance pass him by.

Valdez eyed the others out of the corner of his eyes. He was prepared to share the spoils with them. Fools! They had no idea the money was counterfeit. If they splashed it around, that was their funeral. He intended to move north and lie low for several months until the furore died down. Then he would pass it off to various unsuspecting border rustlers.

In the meantime, General Diaz' revolution would succeed. His masters would be deposed and his disappearance would be forgotten in the euphoria of a great revolutionary victory.

But that was looking ahead. In the meantime, the problem was, where had the woman hidden the money? His men had searched the stage coach very thoroughly, he could testify to that. The portmanteau was her only piece of luggage. He scratched his head thoughtfully.

'Tonight Maria Madelaine will sing at the Black Joke,' Valdez said. 'I think that now we will return to Queensville to hear her performance.'

Garcia stirred uneasily. 'There is a ranger in town,' he muttered.

'He was still firing as we left the plaza,' Manuel said. He took off his sombrero and inspected the bullet hole through it. He shook his head and whistled through his teeth. 'A little lower, and I would have been a dead man.'

'Pah!' Valdez demanded. 'Are we going to let one ranger stand between us and a fortune?'

Garcia scratched his head reflectively. 'Senor, if we rob the woman, cheat Senor Clayton and double-cross General Diaz, we could be in big enough trouble without killing the ranger as well.'

Valdez threw back his head and laughed.

'My friend, you should have thought about that before you agreed to ride with me. But it is up to you. Each of you must make up his mind. If you want to return to Mexico and a lifetime of poverty, do it now.'

Depressed and frustrated as Brad felt about the death of Dan Jasper, he reckoned it would be a mistake to saddle up and ride out after Tilson for he was so certain the young lawman would be back this side of midnight, he'd lay a month's pay on it.

He found a downtown restaurant and ate steak and eggs in solitude. He had plenty to think about. Jake Rauchtenbauer's information, for a start. The saloon owner had come mighty close to being the number one suspect – except that Brad could see no possible motive for his murder of Johnson. Once again it seemed the saloon owner had wriggled out of the net.

Brad pushed his empty plate away and rolled a smoke, his brain working ceaselessly on the possibilities. One thing was plain, Valdez must have known Johnson for what he was. If that was the case, then Valdez himself must be some kind of agent. A Mexican Government agent, perhaps?

Brad pondered until the cigarette stub burned his fingers. He couldn't rid himself of the notion that it was Valdez and his men who'd tried to ride down Tilson and himself back there in the plaza. Why? The average Mexican had no love for a Texas Ranger, he was well aware of that. But that didn't explain the blatant ferocity of the attack. Then they had gone to rob the stage. If that was the case, it was no mere speculation on his part that Colonel Valdez knew Marie Madelaine was bringing in a consignment of money. That being so, he would no doubt soon find out that he hadn't got it.

Which meant that he'd be back!

Brad settled his bill, left the restaurant and stopped by at the telegraph office where he sent a coded message to San Antonio reporting the facts concerning Johnson's death. He did not request further instructions. He knew exactly what McNelly's response would be. As the man on the spot, he was expected to act. If he didn't do something about Johnson's death who would? And if he didn't find out, the whole of South West Texas would soon be crawling with federal agents – which wouldn't please McNelly, as it would reflect on his force's competence as a law-enforcing authority.

As Brad closed the door of the hotel behind him the lobby clerk laid down his pen, and eyed him suspiciously.

'Guess I forgot to check in,' Brad said, his face deadpan. 'The cheapest you've got will do.'

For a moment Brad thought the guy was going to refuse him but fortunately for him he thought the better of it. He pushed the register towards Brad, wrinkling his nose with an air of distaste as though he could smell the scent of death about him.

'Number 16,' the clerk said, sniffing wetly.

'It's on the second floor. Sign the register, please.'

As Brad complied with the request, he scanned the page. There was no mention of Marie Madelaine.

'Have the maid bring me a pitcher of hot water,' Brad told him.

When the coloured chambermaid tapped on his door, he answered it promptly.

'Better service here than in Corpus,' he said genially as she laid the pitcher down on the stand.

Her eyes rolled with pleasure. 'We aim to please, sah,' she replied.

'I understand Miss Madelaine's stayin' here?' he said casually.

'Sure 'ting. She's in number ten. Massa Clayton, he just done left,' the maid said, with a conspiratorial wink as she closed the door.

Just what was Clayton's part in this business?

As he shaved, Brad pondered the problem of how Marie had managed to conceal the money during her journey. After a few moments, the answer came to him with such painful clarity that he almost cut himself.

When he had finished, he drew his shirt back on and sat down on the bed. He pulled out his wallet and took out the two twenty-dollar notes he'd recovered from Johnson. As he pondered, his eyes fell on a copy of the *Queensville Recorder* lying on the dressing table.

The paper carried an account of the recent elections for sheriff. It wasn't a popular job – there had only been two candidates. Although Tilson had evidently been elected by a large majority over his rival, the editorial expressed serious misgivings over the result:

'As good citizens we must bow to democracy but it is debatable as to whether the populace has acted correctly for in our opinion it is debatable as to whether Mr Tilson McCracken's youthful enthusiasm can make up for his lack of experience. The public should have been wary about allowing sympathy for the murder of the father to have influenced the outcome in favour of his son. However, time will tell.'

Brad stopped reading. Right now he had another use for the *Queensville Recorder*...

Taking one of the $20 notes he laid it on the newspaper and with the aid of a stub of pencil made a mark around it. Using his razor, he carefully cut out a rectangle of paper the size of the note. Working with several sheets of newspaper together, in a few moments, he had cut out fifty such pieces.

'Fifty times twenty dollars equals one thousand dollars,' he muttered to himself.

He weighed the bundle speculatively in his palm. It was about the same weight as an ounce of baccy.

Marie Madelaine could easily conceal several thousands of dollars about her person – probably somewhere within her dress.

No wonder her demeanour was so calm on her arrival in Queensville. She might have lost her bag, but he was now certain that she still had the money!

So, he figured he needed urgently to inspect the lady's dress – which could be a mite difficult if she was still wearing it...

For a moment he was mightily tempted to belt on his gun, go along the corridor and arrest her. But caution prevailed. What he needed was evidence – the kind that would stand up in a court of law. Clayton was a man of substance, well-known in Queensville. Chance was he'd got himself mixed up with Marie through falling for her. Brad gave a cynical smile – no doubt Clayton wasn't Marie's first scalp – and he wouldn't be the last.

A sudden commotion in the street drew his attention. He walked across to the window, opened it and looked outside. His room was on the second storey and he had a good view of the group of riders who had drawn to a halt just below him.

The throaty sound of a woman singing in Spanish to the accompaniment of a guitar and the click of castanets clashed incongruously with the snorting of horses and the yapping of several dogs.

'Must be the posse,' Brad muttered to himself. 'Now where the hell has young Tilson got to?'

Suddenly the night air became full of the smell of smoke from newly-rolled cigarettes and the rank odour of sweat from the lathered horses. The moon was full, but looking down from above made it difficult for Brad to spot Tilson, but he could hear what the men were saying.

'We made good time, boys. Say, iffen we're smart about it, maybe we'll just get to hear Marie sing,' a voice said.

A murmur of approval met this.

'Cain't figure out young McCracken. You'da thought he'd have wanted to be back to service that young filly of his, instead of sleuthin',' another man remarked.

A gale of raucous laughter swept through the men, some of whom dismounted and began to disperse across the plaza towards the livery stable, towing their horses after them.

Brad withdrew into the room with a puzzled look on his face. The posse had given up, just like he said it would, but that gave him no satisfaction.

Confound Tilson's hide for being such a hot-headed young idiot! He must have stayed out there hoping he could achieve by himself what a posse had failed to do.

Settling the order of priorities was easy. Tilson would have to wait until morning; if the posse had given up, he must have camped out somewhere on the range and he surely couldn't get into trouble before daylight. In the meantime it was essential for him to keep a check on Marie and Clayton.

He screwed up the bits of mutilated newspaper and dropped them into the wicker basket. If only Johnson had lived! He had a feeling the little detective and himself would have cracked this business wide open very quickly. But it was no use pondering over what might have been.

There was a light tap on his door. Brad walked across and opened it. To his vast surprise, Marie Madelaine was standing outside in the corridor. She was wearing the same dress she had arrived in on the stage three hours earlier.

'Do not look so surprised, *monsieur*,' she said. 'The chambermaid gave me the number of your room.' Her French perfume filled the air with the scent of June roses. 'I am to sing at the Black Joke in half an hour. I need an escort.'

'I guess you've come to the right man,' Brad said as he strapped on his gunbelt.

'I thought I could rely on a ranger,' she said with a winsome smile.

Brad glanced at her out of the corner of his eyes as she took his arm and they stepped out along the corridor together. He was highly aware that this woman did nothing without a motive.

The lobby clerk nearly fell off his stool when he saw Brad escorting Marie Madelaine. Once outside in the darkened street, no one recognised them as they took the short walk across the plaza to the saloon.

'Maybe you'd best go in the back way,' Brad suggested as they drew closer.

Just as he spoke, the bulk of Jake Rauchtenbauer appeared in the pool of yellow light cast by an uncurtained window.

'Oh there you are, Marie!' he exclaimed. 'I was just comin' across to collect you.'

'Do not worry, Jake,' Marie replied. 'Monsieur Saunders offered to escort me and I accepted.'

Brad was aware of the hostility and suspicion in the other man's eyes.

'Will you be staying long in Queensville?' Marie asked Brad.

'Until I complete my investigations.'

'Into what?'

'The passing of counterfeit money,' he replied.

He had taken a calculated risk in revealing his hand and he knew it. Out of the corner of his eyes he observed Rauchtenbauer's startled reaction as easily as he would read a book, but with Marie, he figured he would never get past the cover – and he was right, for the deadpan expression on her face told him nothing.

'The saloon is packed to the doors. I'd better take you round the back way,' Rauchtenbauer said to Marie.

'Very well,' she replied. She turned to acknowledge Brad. 'May I wish you *bonne chance, monsieur* with your investigations.'

Rauchtenbauer's grip tightened on Marie Madelaine's arm as he escorted her away from the dimly lit street into the alley that led to the rear entrance of the Black Joke.

'What the hell are we gonna do, Marie?' he whispered hoarsely as soon as they were out of earshot of the shadowy figure of the ranger. 'That guy's onto you for sure.'

She paused as they reached the door and then rounded on him. 'It is small wonder, with fools like you who give everything away!' Rauchtenbauer recoiled at the venom in her voice. 'That ranger is a very clever man. He told me what he is looking for because he wanted to catch me off my guard. He did not succeed with me, but he read you like a book.'

'But ... but ... what are we gonna do?'

'*You* are going to carry on running your saloon as if nothing has happened. You will do exactly as I say, for remember that it was the deal you did with my brother in El Paso that put you here. Do you understand?'

Rauchtenbauer nodded bleakly. 'Marie, there's somethin' else. When I was on my way here I got mixed up with some guys near the border. I had a chance to double my money on a cattle deal but the local sheriff, a guy called Abe McCracken, was onto it. I was still carrying five grand in my money belt from the deal with your brother when he caught up with me so I filled the sheriff with lead and dropped him in the Rio Grande.'

'Why are you telling me this?' Marie demanded.

'The rangers sent a guy to investigate the sheriff's disappearance. Some busybody found the body. They identified McCracken from his belongings. The ranger came within an ace of pinning it on me, I know it. Saunders has questioned me already, I reckon he could be onto more than just counterfeit money.'

'Then there is only one thing for you to do,' Marie said.

'An' what's that?'

'Keep your nerve,' she replied.

SIX

The noise met Brad like a solid wall as he stepped through the batwings of the Black Joke Saloon.

The sweating, shirt-sleeved barkeep interpreted his lip movement with practised ease as he ordered beer and a bottle and glass came sliding towards him.

With its cut glass chandeliers, solid oak bar and scrolled gilt mirrors, the Black Joke was certainly a cut above the usual western saloon. As Brad took his first pull, he surveyed the room. Jake Rauchtenbauer was sitting at a table, smoking a large cigar and playing cards with a group of local businessmen. There was no sign of Joel Clayton.

'Is Marie singin' tonight?' a cowhand bawled into Brad's ear.

'She's here!'

A roar of approval drowned Brad's reply.

Just as suddenly, the cosmopolitan crowd of cowhands, fishermen, travelling salesmen and small town businessmen gathered round the gaming tables fell silent as Marie Madelaine appeared at the top of the raked staircase leading from the upper gallery onto the newly erected stage.

Not a sound was heard as she laid a black gloved hand on the solid oak balustrade. The pianist vamped a few opening bars and she launched straight into the drinking song from *La Traviata* as she made a slow, step by step descent through the haze of blue smoke hanging across the saloon, smiling into the sea of yearning faces below her as she sang.

Her voice was mature, vigorous yet restrained and she sang without a trace of the maudlin appeal and coyness of many saloon singers. She reached the bottom step and as she finished with her white arms stretched aloft, every glass in the room was raised in a toast as the voice of the audience erupted into a roar of approval.

Marie Madelaine could certainly sing and Brad felt himself borne along on the wave of enthusiasm as a dozen pairs of willing hands reached out and swept her onto the newly built stage. There, arms outstretched, she sang *Home Sweet Home* with such nostalgia that it held her audience dewy eyed and spellbound.

But as Marie sang, Brad noticed her eyes were searching the room. They came to rest on a broad-shouldered, flashily-dressed Mexican, leaning against the wall just inside the door. For a brief second, Brad caught a gleam of recognition in the woman's eyes and a sinister smile on the darkly handsome face of the man.

'More! More!'

When Marie finished singing, the audience whooped, banged their fists on the table, whistled and shouted a chorus of rebel yells that made Brad's hair stand on end. She returned to the foot of the staircase and after acknowledging the applause, she held up her hand for silence. Every eye was focussed on her, every ear strained to listen to what she had to say.

'Please, boys, no more tonight, I've had a long day and I am tired after my journey. I'll sing again for you tomorrow, I promise.'

The audience was aghast.

'Aw Marie, shucks to this operatic stuff, c'mon give us *Dixie!*' a cowboy pleaded.

'Dixie – Dixie – Dixie...'

As the chant grew louder and louder, Marie's glittering smile ignited every world-weary face in the room. She held up her hand and the room fell silent once more.

'Please, boys, I'm tired...'

'Goldarn it, sing it, Miss Marie, sing! Sing fer all those brave boys who are sleeping forever.'

The room fell silent as Clem Partridge staggered forward. He was three parts drunk but he was speaking from the heart and everyone knew it. Before he reached the stage, the grinning Jake Rauchtenbauer grabbed the old-timer by the scruff of his neck and hauled him back.

'Very well, then I shall sing *Dixie* for you.'

Marie waited until the rebel yells had died away. Then, with consummate timing she nodded to the pianist and began to sing. As he joined in the chorus, Brad felt emotion he had buried deep down inside these last few years rising once more. For him, like thousands of others who had endured the bitterness of losing the war and the misery of the Reconstruction, Dixie lived on. So great was the effect on him that several moments had elapsed after she had finished singing before he realised that Marie had disappeared – and so had the Mexican.

'Ain't she just the greatest singer you ever heard?' a hulking teamster enthused as Brad thrust his way towards the door through the excited throng.

And he was compelled to agree.

On the upper floor of the Black Joke Saloon, Joel Clayton paced the carpeted floor of Marie's dressing room, both hands clasped behind his back. Not even the muffled deep-throated roars of approval from the saloon were sufficient to interrupt his preoccupation. Jake Rauchtenbauer had given up his own room for Marie Madelaine. Lamplight from a chandelier bathed the brocaded drapes, the huge bed, plush chairs and carved tables in a soft yellow bloom. But the opulence of his surroundings was lost on the preoccupied Clayton.

Where the hell was Valdez?

He had spent nearly an hour in the hotel

lobby waiting for the Mexican, but he had failed to turn up. Until he met him, it was impossible to complete the deal for he had no idea where Valdez was holding the herd. One hundred bloodstock bulls could be hidden anywhere along the wild mesquite brakes bordering the Rio Grande.

He'd heard mention from various sources that Valdez had ridden into town earlier that day, but now he was nowhere to be found. Word was that he and his men had tried to ride down young McCracken and the ranger in the plaza. What the hell was he playing at? Something had gone badly wrong, he could feel it in his bones. As he paused to light a cigar, the door of the room burst open.

'Why Marie, you've finished early!' he exclaimed. 'Don't you feel well tonight?' Marie pushed away his clumsy attempt to embrace her. She closed the door and walked over to a low table, poured herself a glass of champagne and downed it in a gulp.

'This is the last time I shall sing in a place like this, I swear,' she said vehemently after clearing her throat.

'Is there something wrong?' Clayton asked her.

With difficulty, she regained control of her heaving bosom. 'I do not like being so close to the audience,' she complained. 'Jake Rauchtenbauer gave me the impression I was to perform in an opera house, not a cheap gambling saloon.'

'Gee, Marie, I'm sorry,' Clayton said with genuine humility. 'But I guess this is the best we can do in these parts. I'm sure Jake has gone to a lot of trouble to build a stage for you. One day we'll have the best opera house in the south west, I promise you that.'

Marie sat down on the edge of the four poster bed. Clayton shifted uncomfortably as she stared at him.

'So how did your meeting go with Valdez?'

Her voice sounded so low and venomous that despite the warm atmosphere Clayton felt a cold sweat start under his armpits.

'He didn't show. I waited over an hour. I don't understand it, he's never missed out on a meeting with me before.'

'Ah, now I understand,' Marie said in a low voice. She walked across to the door and turned the key. 'I have to get away from here,' she said urgently.

'Why?'

'Colonel Valdez was out there in the audience tonight.'

Clayton's eyebrows raised. 'I didn't know you knew him?'

Marie's eyes narrowed. Her mouth twisted into a cynical smile. 'I first met him this afternoon.'

'I don't understand. There was no one else on that stage except you.'

'He wasn't on the stage, *cheri*...'

Clayton stared at her in amazement. 'You think it was Valdez who robbed you?'

Marie nodded.

'How can you be sure of that? According to the driver those *ladrones* were wearing bandannas over their faces.'

'A woman has only to see the eyes of a man, *cheri* and she can read all she needs to know in them.'

Clayton looked puzzled. 'Why should Valdez want to take the money off you before we do the deal?'

Marie gave a cynical smile. 'With men like Valdez you must always be on your guard. It is clear that he intended to take the money for himself.'

'Renege on the deal? Why, the lousy, double-crossin' sonofabitch!' Clayton exploded. He thrust his hand inside his jacket, withdrew a .38 calibre suicide special from a shoulder holster and checked it.

Marie drew closer to him and held his arm. 'Be calm, *cheri*. I still have the money, but we can't stay here. Not with Valdez and his men around. Why not take me out to your ranch? We will be safe there.'

'Why should I run away from a lousy greaser?' Clayton sneered. He started for the door.

Marie restrained him. '*Cheri*, you do not understand. Valdez knows exactly what he is doing. He will kill you if you go out there.'

Clayton's face went pale under his tan. He shook his head in bewilderment. 'I don't understand, I thought your brother and me were doing a straight business deal with Valdez.'

'He was – until Valdez changed his mind.'

'I still think you're wrong about this,' Clayton said. 'I guess I'd better tell Jake right-away.'

Before Marie could reply, there was a knock at the door. Clayton cocked the suicide special and approached it circumspectly.

'Who is it?' he called softly.

'Jake Rauchtenbauer,' came the reply.

Clayton opened the door to let the owner of the Black Joke into the room and closed it again.

'Well?'

Rauchtenbauer's expression was grim. 'Valdez is askin' to see you, Joel. He's got a bunch of guys with him who look real mean. My boys are eyeballin' 'em off at the moment. Look, I don't want no bust-ups, I just spent a fortune on this place. If you've got a quarrel with Valdez, it's better if you sort it out elsewhere.'

'So you were right, Marie,' Clayton exclaimed.

Rauchtenbauer eyed the couple curiously. 'I gotta tell you, the ranger came quizzin' round earlier on. He's got Valdez in the frame for murderin' Dan Jasper and shooting that guy Johnson over at the hotel.'

Marie rounded on him. 'Did you say Johnson?' she exclaimed.

'Yeah, say Marie what the hell is goin' on?'

Marie's mouth tightened to a hyphen. 'Eli Johnson worked as an agent for the US Government. I know he's been following me, but I thought I had given him the slip this time.'

Rauchtenbauer stared at Marie and Clayton. 'Valdez was your contact this time?'

Clayton nodded. 'Marie's carrying one hundred grand.'

'Hell's teeth!' Rauchtenbauer ejaculated. 'What does Valdez want with that kinda money? Is he trying to finance the whole damn Mexican Revolution?'

'Somethin' like that,' Clayton agreed. 'But we ain't got time to discuss it now. Marie's life's in danger. We gotta get her outa here – fast.'

'Hey wait a minute, you ain't thinkin' of leavin'? You've signed a contract to sing here, there's gonna be a riot if you don't,' Rauchtenbauer protested. 'My boys can see off Valdez and his boys, no problem.'

'Strange isn't it?' Clayton said. 'A moment ago you were talking about protectin' this place. The minute a hundred grand is mentioned you change your tune.'

Rauchtenbauer smiled rapaciously. 'Money talks. That deal I did with the marquis in El Paso set me up here in Queensville. A hundred grand could set me up in an opera house in Galveston.'

Clayton jabbed his suicide special into Rauchtenbauer's ribs. 'Don't go gettin' yourself any big ideas,' he growled. 'You just get Marie an' me outa here.'

At that moment, a shot rang out...

Valdez' attempt to big-talk his way into the Black Joke Saloon had failed to impress the two taciturn muscleheads guarding the rear entrance. Their previous unpleasant experience with Brad had triggered a knee-jerk reaction to subsequent encounters which they now took the precaution of backing up with Colts held in each hairy fist. Colonel Valdez conducted a strategic withdrawal of his men into the alley in order to consider his next move.

'I do not think they are expecting any more trouble from us,' Garcia said. 'Suppose I climb onto the roof, get into the upper storey and take them from the rear?'

Valdez clapped Garcia on the shoulder so forcefully he staggered. 'Good idea!' he exclaimed. 'We will start a disturbance out here in the alley that will keep them busy while you make the attempt.'

Valdez deployed Pedro and Manuel on either side of the entrance and then took up a position at one end of the alley from which he had a good view of Garcia's tapering silhouette as he progressed cat-like along the roof. As soon as Garcia reached one of the windows, he opened fire.

He must get to Marie Madelaine before Valdez.
That thought was uppermost in Brad's mind as he slipped out of the batwing doors of the Black Joke Saloon and out into the plaza. A cool breeze was blowing in from the sea making the atmosphere clean and fresh

after the thick atmosphere inside the saloon. There was no way he could follow Marie up the staircase, for the minute she disappeared the way was blocked by the hired muscle. As the last thing he wanted to do was to draw attention to himself, his only hope was to gain entrance from the rear.

He walked along the clap-board false frontage and then turned into the side alley he figured led to the rear of the saloon. As he edged in closer, he cursed his earlier lack of vigilance. But like everyone else in the saloon he had allowed himself to be dazzled by Marie's overpowering physical attraction.

It was dark in the alley. A cat scrambled over a trash bin rattling the lid as it did so. A sudden awareness told him he wasn't alone. A scrabbling noise above him attracted his attention.

A man was crawling along the roof of the saloon!

To his right he heard a soft footfall and caught a brief sighting of a shadowy figure merging into the deep shadows at the far end of the alley.

Brad froze, glancing all the while about him. Something was happening, but he didn't have a clue what it was all about.

Suddenly, from being the quietest place in Texas, the alley echoed to the sound of a shot ringing out and a bullet fanned his cheek.

As he flung himself to the ground, a cloud scurried across the pale-faced moon and suddenly the peace of the night turned into a nightmare of shouting, scurrying, shadowy figures and stabbing spits of flame. Brad found himself in the middle of a hail of bullets which seemed to come from all directions. He snapped a shot with his Peacemaker at the silhouette of the man on the roof and his accuracy was rewarded with a cry of pain.

But in the confines of the alley lead hummed, ricocheting from all directions, slicing splinters of wood off the buildings and sparking off the trash bin until one struck Brad a glancing blow on the side of the head and his consciousness disintegrated into a shower of brilliant, red-hot sparks...

When he came round, Brad felt gingerly at the lump on the back of his aching head. Slowly his vision cleared. There was no blood on his fingers, his battered stetson must have prevented the skin of his scalp from breaking.

The gunfight was over. The alley was deserted. Brad rose to his feet, found a trough and sluiced water over his head until his double vision cleared leaving a tiny ache behind his eyes. He waited awhile but no one appeared. The alley cat sat on the overturned trash bin watching him intently for a few seconds before it resumed licking its paws as though nothing had happened to disturb the peace.

Brad rolled a smoke and finished it before resuming his unfinished business.

'Where d'you think you're goin'?' the hired muscle guarding the rear entrance to the Black Joke Saloon demanded. He jabbed his gun so hard into Brad's ribs, it made him gasp. Brad's temper snapped and in the pitch dark of the doorway, the man failed to see the knee driving deep into his groin. He crumpled over with a gasp of agony, his gun clattering to the floor.

Brad stepped over the inert body and entered the saloon. Through the doors ahead of him he could hear the hubbub of the sweating crowd within.

A steep flight of stairs led off to his left. A sputtering oil lamp just provided enough illumination to see. He climbed the stairs and paused at the top to take in his bearings.

To his right he could see the gallery from which Marie had made her dramatic entrance to the stage below. A gale of raucous laughter rose from the saloon below. Somewhere along here, Marie Madelaine must have a dressing room.

A pool of yellow light shone through the half-open door of Rauchtenbauer's office. He kicked the door open with his foot and stepped inside.

'What the hell's goin' on?'

Jake Rauchtenbauer started up from his desk, scattering neat piles of the evening's takings.

'You tell me,' Brad drawled.

Rauchtenbauer sank slowly back into his chair when he recognised Brad.

'Where is Marie Madelaine?' Brad demanded.

Rauchtenbauer shrugged his big shoulders. 'How should I know?'

Brad planted both hands on the desk and brought his nose one inch from Rauchtenbauer's.

'There was gunplay out the back just now. Before a bullet slugged me I saw a guy crawling along your roof. Any idea who they were?'

Rauchtenbauer shrugged. 'How should I

know? It's dark out there. OK, so a few guys get drunk and try to get to Marie Madelaine. It ain't no big deal. It happens everywhere. My boys saw 'em off – that's what I pay 'em for. I reckon the guy on the roof got hit by one of his own men.' He caught sight of Brad's blood-flecked shirt collar. 'Too bad if you got caught in the middle of it, you should mind how you go. Marie left here once the fracas was over.'

'With who?'

'Joel Clayton, I guess.'

'So he was here in the saloon while Marie was singin'?'

Rauchtenbauer nodded.

'Any idea where they went?'

'Why, Marie's staying over at the hotel. You know that. I guess Joel came over to escort her back there. If they've got somethin' goin' between 'em, it ain't my affair. Marie has a big reputation as a singer. So long as she keeps her contract, I got no quarrel with her on that account.'

SEVEN

Brad left the Black Joke by the front entrance. As he crossed the plaza he kept careful watch about him. If Rauchtenbauer was telling the truth – and as far as he was concerned there was no need for him to do otherwise, Colonel Valdez and his men had made a determined effort to get to Marie Madelaine and the money. The attempt had failed and Joel Clayton had spirited her away.

The lobby clerk at the hotel was as misanthropic as ever.

'I am not at liberty to reveal Miss Madelaine's movements,' he said. 'I am sure she would expect me to respect her privacy.'

'Mister, I ain't got time to mind your conscience, even iffen I thought you had one. I guess I'll go up and kick the door down,' Brad told him bluntly.

The lobby clerk's face turned the colour of whitewash. 'There's no need to do that,' he told Brad. 'I have Miss Madelaine's key right here. She hasn't returned since she left

123

here earlier with you.'

Brad cursed Jake Rauchtenbauer for a timewaster as he left the hotel and made his way to the livery stable. A whiff of fresh dung mingled with hay, grain and dust met him as he opened the barn door. Inside, there was nothing to be heard except the snorting of a horse.

At first, he saw nothing except the shadowy shapes of the animals sleeping in the stalls. No one was sitting behind the roll topped desk in the glass fronted office. As he looked round, suddenly he became aware of the pale face of a boy peering at him from the hay loft.

'Hey, boy! Why are you hiding up there?' Brad called out.

'*Buenos tardes, senor,*' the boy said. He descended the ladder, holding a lantern, squinting at Brad in the dim yellow light. 'Have you come to see your fine horse? I take care of him real good for you.'

Brad recognised the young Mexican from earlier on that day when he had stabled Blaze. He followed the boy along the central aisle until he drew level with the stall holding the big bay. The horse rose to its feet instantly and whickered a welcome as Brad drew near.

'He ees big big horse, very strong,' the youngster opined as he patted Blaze's muzzle with an authoritative air.

Brad flipped his Durham sack from his top left hand vest pocket, rolled a cigarette and lit it.

'What's your name, boy?' Brad asked.

'Pedro Gonzales.'

'Well now, Pedro, have you had anyone else in here tonight?'

'Sure t'ing,' Pedro nodded eagerly. 'Senor Clayton and the beautiful senorita. I harness the horses to a buckboard for them and they leave town.'

'And where do you reckon Senor Clayton and his beautiful senorita are headin' on this fine moonlight night?' Brad asked.

The boy's teeth flashed in a smile. 'I t'ink maybe they go to his ranch, *senor*.'

'The Lazy Z?'

'*Si, senor*.'

'Fetch my saddle,' Brad said abruptly.

Pedro looked at Brad curiously. 'You will follow them, tonight, *senor*?'

Brad did not reply. He waited while Pedro opened the gate of the stall and led Blaze out into the aisle.

The boy grunted as he hefted the forty pound saddle into position and stepped aside to allow Brad to tighten the double cinches to his own satisfaction. When he was ready, Brad led Blaze to the door. He paused with one foot in the stirrup.

'How do I get to the Lazy Z?' he asked abruptly.

'It ees 'bout four hours' easy ride. The trail, she lead north east straight to it from town. It ees big and wide. No problem for a buckboard. You will find it easily, *senor*, even in the dark.'

'How long is it since they left?'

'Half an hour, maybe.'

Brad rose into the saddle. It was just after midnight. If Clayton was taking Marie out to his ranch, he could follow at his leisure, take an hour's rest and ride in at dawn. He fumbled in one of his vest pockets and tossed the boy a quarter.

'You tell no one where I have gone – understand?' he said.

'*Comprendo. Muchas graçias, senor.*'

'*Hasta la vista.*'

'Wait, *senor*, there is something else you should know.'

Brad held Blaze and looked down at the boy.

'Another man, he come here also. Like you, he is asking about *Senor* Clayton and the *senorita*.'

Brad leaned forward in the saddle. 'What kinda man was he, Pedro?'

'He is *ladrone*. Very bad. I have seen him before. He rides with General Diaz to make revolution. He carry no guns, just two knives. He say he will cut my throat if I do not tell heem where *Senor* Clayton and the *senorita* went.' Pedro crossed himself devoutly. 'So I tell him. He did not pay me.'

'Were there any others with him?'

'Three. I see him meet them at the end of the street. One of them is Colonel Valdez.'

Valdez!

The situation had changed once more. If Clayton and Marie couldn't reach the safety of the Lazy Z before the Mexican caught up with them, they were in big trouble.

'*Muchas graçias,*' Brad said.

'*Senor*, if you see them, you will not tell them what I have said to you?' Pedro said anxiously. 'They will kill me if they find out.'

'Don't you worry none, boy,' Brad replied and with an imperceptible touch of his lightly spurred heels he eased Blaze into a canter along the narrow street.

Out on the trail to the Lazy Z, Colonel Valdez came to a halt, held up his arm and waited for his men to join him. As Garcia eased his horse alongside him he took time to tighten the bloodstained bandanna he'd tied round the bloody furrow in his left arm with a grimace.

'Only the ranger can shoot like that. He must have eyes like a cat,' he said morosely.

'Well, let us make sure we catch up with Marie Madelaine and Joel Clayton before he does,' Valdez replied as he surveyed the land ahead.

'I thought you said you had hit him?'

'I would not swear to it, but I thought I saw a man drop in the alley.'

'Senor Rauchtenbauer used his men to help them to get away,' Valdez said softly. 'I shall not forget that.'

'They will hear us coming if we get too close,' Garcia said.

Valdez cocked one eye at the full moon. 'And see us, as well. We herded cattle this way a few weeks ago. The trail takes a wide sweep to the north east. You follow the way ahead with Manuel. Ride carefully, do not get too close and alarm them. Pedro and I will ride across country and intercept them.'

Valdez and his *compadre* eased their mounts off the trail and began to force their way across the trackless range. After half an hour of hard riding, they hit the broad trail once more.

'We are too late, I think,' Pedro commented as they stared at the deserted track.

'Ssh!' Valdez held up his hand for silence.

In the distance they heard the sound of approaching horses. The two men eased their horses forward into the middle of the trail and held their ground as the buckboard appeared. Clayton was holding the reins with Marie Madelaine sitting beside him. For a brief second, it appeared as if Clayton was going to make a run for it, but he thought the better of it and brought the buckboard to a standstill.

'What the hell are you up to, Valdez?' Clayton demanded. 'I thought we had a deal.'

'I think you know very well what it is I want, *senor*,' Valdez replied.

'But what about the deal?' Clayton insisted.

'It is still on, *senor*, but the terms have changed,' Valdez said.

At that moment, Garcia and Pedro appeared behind Clayton.

'Hey, now what is this?' Clayton exclaimed.

'Eet is OK, *senor*. Do not concern yourself. Now if the *senorita* will just hand over the money.'

Marie Madelaine returned Valdez' smile. 'I see you have the advantage this time, *monsieur*,' she said.

Colonel Valdez stirred uneasily. The woman's complete lack of fear unnerved him.

'Come!' he urged. 'Let us not waste any more time. Last time you duped me. This time – no.'

Marie Madelaine half turned in her seat and indicated the well of the buckboard behind her. 'It is here, *monsieur*. In these saddlebags. One hundred thousand dollars for General Diaz.'

Valdez ignored the sarcastic edge to her voice as he nodded to Garcia, who urged his horse forward to the side of the buckboard. He leaned over and grabbed the saddlebags with a cry of triumph.

'Please, *monsieur*, you check it is there. I do not wish to waste any more of your time,' Marie said.

'Why, Marie, what are you thinkin' of?' Clayton cried.

Garcia opened one of the saddlebags and plunged his hand inside. He retrieved a bundle and threw it across to Valdez. With trembling hands, Valdez struck a lucifer and inspected it.

'Is it right this time?' Garcia asked him.

Valdez' face exploded into a grin. 'One note for twenty dollars,' he said. Hastily he counted the rest of the bundle. 'One, two, three, four ... fifty notes for twenty dollars...'

'Is one thousand dollars,' Garcia said with a smile which would have graced a cherubim.

Valdez grabbed the bags off him and flourished them high. 'One hundred thousand dollars!' he exclaimed triumphantly. 'Let's go!'

Valdez slammed the saddle bags across his pommel. As he did so, Clayton spotted his momentary distraction and seized his chance. His hand went for the suicide special in his shoulder holster.

'No, Joel!' Marie Madelaine screamed as she saw Garcia's lightning reaction.

There was a hissing noise and flash of steel as one of Garcia's knives struck Clayton in the chest. The suicide special's slug disappeared skywards as Marie Madelaine caught hold of him but failed to prevent him slumping backwards into the well of the buckboard.

'*Adios, amigos!*' Valdez whirled his horse round and led his men at a fast gallop away from the trail.

Brad eased Blaze out of Queensville. By the stars he found the broad trail leading north east without difficulty and followed it at a fast lope in the stillness of the moonlit night. Suddenly he heard the sound of a faint scream followed immediately by a shot.

Valdez must have caught up with Clayton and Marie!

He touched Blaze's flanks lightly and the big bay surged forward in a mile-eating gallop which ten minutes later brought him to a bend in the trail beyond which he came upon Marie kneeling in the buckboard beside the prostrate body of Joel Clayton.

'So, it is you, *monsieur*,' Marie said.

Once again Brad was taken aback by the woman's total self-possession. It was almost as if she had been expecting him. What the hell was going on? This whole business was beginning to irritate him, he had a nasty feeling that matters were careering completely beyond his control.

He bent down over the injured man and saw he was hurt bad. The knife had entered his right side. It must have touched the lung, for as Clayton gave a slight cough, his spittle was tinged with blood.

'What happened?' Brad asked, straight-

132

ening up.

'A man called Garcia did this to him,' Marie replied calmly. 'One of Colonel Valdez' men.'

'Why should he do this?'

'I think perhaps he wanted to rob us.'

You bet your life he did! Brad thought grimly.

'Do you know this man, Valdez?'

'I never saw him before in my life.'

It was a superb performance. With an effort, Brad tore himself away from her spell. He had been fed many a pack of lies in his time. How much of this story was he supposed to believe?

But one thing still puzzled him – once again, Marie wasn't behaving as though she had just lost a large sum of money!

'How many men did Valdez have with him?'

'Three – but we are wasting time. Joel needs a doctor. Will you help me to take him back to Queensville?'

Brad pondered. If Valdez had taken the money, by the time he had taken Clayton into town, he and his men would be well on their way to the border.

But what else could he do? Whatever Marie was, she was a woman – and a woman could not be left alone deep in this inhospitable countryside without an escort. That apart from the wounded Clayton, whom common humanity wouldn't allow him to leave without trying his best to get him medical help.

'Well, *monsieur?*'

As she laid a hand, feather-light on his arm and her eyes locked with his, Brad could feel the sensuality of Marie's presence and inwardly cursed the subtlety and power of her persuasion.

Dawn was beginning to streak the sky as he bent over the injured man. The knife would have to come out, Clayton would never stand the journey with it still implanted in his body. Taking a deep breath, Brad took the hilt between his thumb and forefinger and tweaked it out. Clayton coughed slightly, his spittle was flecked with blood.

Brad sat back on his haunches and scratched his head. It didn't look good. Marie, all the while, had watched him impassively. Her equanimity irritated Brad, it was as though she was calling the shots all the time.

'So what will we do now, *monsieur?*' she enquired.

'Best get you both back to town,' Brad said.

He jumped down from the buckboard and retrieved Blaze. He gathered the reins and led the animal to the tail of the buckboard with the intention of tethering him there. As he did so, a slight fluttering caught his eye.

Puzzled, he bent down to investigate. It looked like a rumpled piece of paper. He picked it up and inspected it in the strengthening light.

It was a banknote!

Fortunately he was out of Marie's line of vision. He stuffed the note into the lower pocket of his vest. Then he finished the job of tethering Blaze and climbed into the seat of the buckboard.

The sun was just nudging above the horizon as Brad shook the reins and the buckboard jerked gently into motion. He held the horses to walking pace in order to minimise the effect on the wounded Clayton who was barely conscious and when he was, he babbled feverish inanities. At the rate they were travelling, Brad figured they wouldn't make Queensville until mid-afternoon...

Tilson had spent an uneasy night on the floor of the living room. At first light he was awoken by the padding of Renata's bare feet as she set about the task of preparing breakfast.

Tilson rose and raked the ashes of the fire before adding a few sticks of mesquite to bring about a miniature version of the conflagration he had witnessed the night before. That done he went outside to draw water from the pump for a wash. On the horizon, the fire on the range was still burning and an ugly plume of smoke coiled upwards to blot out the sun. As he pumped water into a bucket, stripped off his shirt and began his ablutions he became aware that the girl was watching him. She threw him a towel and viewed his slab muscled body with a healthy interest as he dried himself off.

'What you gonna do, Tilson?' she asked him as he pulled on his flannel shirt and fastened the buttons.

Her casual manner astonished him. 'What kinda question is that?' he said. 'Surely you gotta be thinkin' 'bout your own future?'

'That don't take no doin',' the girl said. 'Ma's made her mind up. With pa dead, there ain't no cause for us to be staying here. We're quittin'.'

'I'm mighty relieved to hear that,' Tilson replied. He glanced back at the fire as he spoke. 'Your ma's right, there ain't no livin' to be earned right here, not nohow.'

The girl took the towel off him. 'Ma's askin' a favour of you,' she said boldly.

'What's that?' Tilson asked.

'We're gonna head fer Queensville. She has a cousin there. He's a fisherman. Lives on his own. Always had a soft spot fer him, I reckon. She figures we could stay with him awhile. She thought maybe you could keep us company 'til we got there.'

Tilson hesitated. What he really wanted to do was jump on his horse and ride after those *ladrones*. What a feather in his cap it would be if he caught them! It would show that Texas Ranger just how well he knew his sleuthin'...

But right now he was facing a situation he could hardly ignore since he was in part responsible for what had happened.

'I told ma there wasn't any need fer you to put yourself about,' the girl said with a proud toss of her head. 'I'll take care of her. I guess I can handle a rifle as well as any man.'

Tilson didn't hesitate any longer. His innate sense of responsibility overrode any other consideration. Queensville was only a couple of hours' ride and if any harm befell the girl and her mother, on their journey through this bandit-infested country, he would never be able to live with himself.

'OK,' he said. 'I'll ride with you.'

The girl's eyes brightened. 'I'll go tell ma rightaway,' she said. 'Say, would ya mind catchin' the chickens fer me?'

They arrived in Queensville mid-morning. Renata, cradling a Winchester in her lap, was sitting beside her mother who held the reins of the two horses drawing the buckboard. Tilson rode alongside. A dozen chickens squawked and cackled inside their makeshift coops piled on top of the rest of the family's belongings. A large mongrel ran point, its nose to the ground and a cow, lowing cantankerously, her udders swollen with milk, lumbered reluctantly behind, tethered to the tail of the buckboard.

Their circus-style arrival was observed with mirth by members of the male population lounging on the sidewalks. Some of them had ridden with Tilson in the aborted posse the day before.

Among them was Jake Rauchtenbauer.

'Hey Tilson, boy, you go out chasin' *ladrones* and you done found yourself a wife!' he shouted. 'Boy, you sure know how to pick a good-lookin' gal.'

A titter of laughter greeted this sally.

Tilson glowered. 'There ain't no cause for you to insult this young lady,' he snapped.

'Say, are you cheatin' on Victoria Clayton? Maybe you should leave her to a real man. I never could reckon on what she saw in a guy like you,' Rauchtenbauer jeered. 'Mark you, this new little mare looks a real goer...'

Something snapped inside Tilson. He dismounted and strode up the steps of the sidewalk to confront his tormentor.

Rauchtenbauer stepped forward.

'C'mon city-boy, this is a man's world. Let's see how you make out in a real rough house,' he sneered.

'Why, Jake Rauchtenbauer, I guess I owe you one for Renata,' Tilson said softly.

Before Rauchtenbauer could move, Tilson's arm cycled back and forth with the power of a locomotive connecting rod. The air was filled with the low whistles of the onlookers as Tilson's balled fist sank deep into Rauchtenbauer's fleshy paunch one inch above his gunbelt. He doubled over, his breathing coming in great whooping gasps as his diaphragm went into a temporary spasm induced by the force of the blow and he sank to his knees.

'Gawd almighty, he's bin an' gone an'

flattened 'im!' Luke Pettigrew shouted.

Tilson returned to his horse and mounted it.

'Let's go,' he said to Renata's mother.

'Tilson!' Renata shouted.

Tilson whirled round to see Rauchtenbauer lurching down the steps of the saloon. His breathing was still coming in great gasps but now his right hand was hovering ominously over the butt of the Navy Colt strapped to his waist.

A shot echoed across the plaza, dispersing a flock of pigeons. Rauchtenbauer flung himself flat on the ground as a slug whined past his head and splintered the doorjamb of the Black Joke Saloon.

'Don't even think of it, mister,' Renata said coolly, lowering her Winchester.

Looking up at the smoking barrel of the rifle had a dramatically calming effect on Rauchtenbauer, for something in the tone of the girl's voice told him she would shoot him if she had to.

'I guess you needed a woman to bail you out,' he sneered at Tilson.

Renata's mother cracked the whip. 'Hup, hup!' she shouted and the buckboard jerked forward.

'What the hell did you do that for?' Tilson

raged at Renata as they rode away. 'I could've handled that situation myself...'

'Pa thought that way, too – and look what happened to him,' the girl flashed back at him. 'Anyway, there was no need to stand up fer me, I know I'm no oil painting.'

Tilson lapsed into an angry silence.

When they arrived on the quay, Tilson helped the family to unload the buckboard outside the wooden house which overlooked the tiny harbour. The job done, he made to leave.

'Say, what you plannin' on doin'?' the girl asked him as he unhitched his horse.

He scratched his head. To tell the truth he was plumb out of ideas. Reluctantly he conceded that maybe he ought to contact Ranger Saunders.

'Ain't you gonna ride after those *ladrones?*'

The girl's tough talk irritated Tilson. It was all very well, but where did he start looking?

'I guess I'd better call back at the office. There may be a message for me,' he said lamely.

'Mind if I tag along?'

Tilson stared at the girl.

'Shouldn't you stay here with your ma?'

Renata shrugged. 'Why should I? I reckon she don't need me around. She's too busy mendin' her own life.'

'But I got work to do.'

'So? Maybe you'll be needin' a deputy.'

'I can't deputise you – you're a woman!' Tilson exclaimed.

The girl tilted her sombrero back and gazed frankly at him. 'Who backed you up just now when that bum all but drew on you? Not one of the townsfolk, that's fer sure – an' they elected you. Now see here, Tilson, I saw my pa murdered and I want justice for the guy who did it – an' I'm gonna ride with anyone who's headin' in his direction.'

'I guess you're talkin' plain stupid,' Tilson said. But inside he felt admiration for the girl. After all, they shared a common cause – to seek out the murderers of their respective fathers.

'I've said my piece,' he said resignedly. 'I ain't gonna argue with you no more.'

Tilson bestrode his horse and eased along the street. As he passed the Livery Stable, a loud 'hssst' came from the doorway.

As Tilson dismounted, little Pedro Gonzales beckoned to him.

'*Senor*, late last night those men who shoot at you yesterday in the plaza, they come back to town.'

'You sure?'

'*Si, senor.* One of them he come here last night.' Pedro drew the edge of his hand across his throat and his eyes bulged in a dramatic gesture. 'He say he will kill me if I do not tell him where *Senor* Clayton and the *senorita* has gone.'

'Where have they gone?'

'To the Lazy Z.'

'Do you know where the ranger is?'

Pedro hesitated. The quarter Brad had given him still lay safe in his pocket. But the prospect of a little more interest on his capital drove him on.

'Tell us, Pedro, we need to know.'

Tilson whirled round. 'Renata! I thought I told you not to follow me...'

'It's a free country, you cain't stop me,' the girl replied. 'I'll go where I wanna go.' She turned her attention back to Pedro. 'What else do you know?'

'Is nothing to tell, *senorita* except that these men they all ride out of town.'

Tilson remounted his horse. 'Thanks, Pedro,' he said.

'You will not say I told you, *senor?*' Pedro said anxiously. 'Only the ranger, he pay me for telling him...'

Realisation dawned on Tilson. He

scrabbled in his pocket and tossed the boy a quarter. 'So did the ranger follow them?'

'*Si, senor.*'

Renata drew alongside him.

'So, the trail leads to the Lazy Z?'

'Listen Renata, how many times do I have to tell you? I don't want it you should ride with me!' Tilson exploded.

'OK, but if I don't ride with you, I'll follow on behind,' the girl replied. 'You're brand new to this kinda thing. Any fool can see that. You need someone to keep an eye on you. Whatever, two pairs of eyes are better than one.'

'OK,' Tilson said, shaking his head in weary resignation.

EIGHT

Brad rode beside Marie, turning occasionally to glance at the wounded Clayton. He kept their progress along the trail to a walking pace, trying to minimise the jolting of the buckboard. Although they were only a couple of hours of normal riding out of town, he was taking no chances. All the while he was itching to compare the banknote he had found with a genuine one. If it was counterfeit he was certain that Valdez and his gang had got clean away with the money.

'It is fortunate that you were following us,' Marie told him. She slipped her arm inside Brad's as she spoke. 'One of Valdez' men heard you coming and they left quickly. But tell me, why were you riding out to the Lazy Z at that time of night?'

'Why, that was the very same question I wanted to ask you, Marie,' Brad replied.

She held up a slim finger. 'Psst! I hear someone coming!'

Brad glanced at her out of the corner of his eye. Western girls prided themselves on being of tougher fibre than their Eastern counterparts, but this Frenchwoman was a breed all her own, totally in command of herself; and what was more, she seemed to have a sixth sense for danger. She must have been one hell of a spy to elude a sleuth like Eli Johnson.

They were approaching a bend in the trail. Brad reined in the buckboard. There was little point in taking cover, for the injured man could not be moved hastily. As he withdrew his Peacemaker, out of the corner of his eye he noticed Marie was keeping behind him; it was almost as though she was using him as a screen.

Brad spotted the two approaching riders first.

'Tilson! Where the hell have you been?' he snapped as the couple rounded the corner.

'Well, now, I guess I've been looking out for you,' Tilson said shamefacedly.

'So the posse gave up?'

He nodded. 'Just like you said it would.'

Brad twirled his gun on its trigger guard and replaced it in its holster. He could see the boy was riled enough without him harping on it. As his eye settled on Tilson's youthful looking companion his expression became thunderous.

'Who's this? Fer a guy who's out ridin', you certainly know how to choose your company,' he said.

Marie Madelaine smiled as Tilson flushed to the roots of his hair. But Renata eased her horse forward, her eyes blazing with anger.

'You got it all wrong, Mr Ranger-man,' she said hotly. 'Me and Tilson are out lookin' fer a guy who's murdered my father.'

Brad stared at the girl. Dressed in men's clothing, she looked as tough an example of the opposite sex as he'd seen in a while. But she was still young, the experience of passing years hadn't left its mark on her yet.

'*You* an' Tilson?' he said harshly. He rounded on Tilson. 'What are you thinkin' of? Since when has a sheriff ever deputised a woman to help chase a murderer?'

'But me and Renata...' Tilson began.

'Shut up!' Brad snapped.

His angry voice roused the wounded Clayton who stirred in the well of the buckboard and groaned. With an effort Brad regained control of his temper. Tilson looked so crestfallen he almost felt sorry for him. But there was no more time for recrimination, right now he needed help if he were to deal effectively with Valdez and his men.

Brad drew Tilson and Renata out of earshot of Marie.

'Tell me what happened,' he said to them. 'An' make it snappy, we ain't got time to waste.'

He fished out his Durham sack and fashioned a smoke, listening in silence while Tilson told his story and with rising anger as Renata filled in her part of events with an accurate description of Valdez and his men.

'It's the same gang we're after, Brad, for sure,' Tilson concluded. Brad nodded. He glanced back over his shoulder at the buckboard. 'How long will it take to get this man into town?' he snapped.

Tilson looked doubtfully at the stretcher. 'It's about an hour of normal ridin', but it's gonna take twice as long, I reckon, the state he's in.'

'So here's what we're gonna do.' Brad jumped down from the buckboard, released Blaze and climbed into the saddle. 'Tilson, I want you to ride with me...'

'If you're trailin' those *ladrones*, I'm comin', too,' Renata said stoutly.

'Oh no, you ain't,' Brad said firmly. 'You're gonna assume responsibility for getting Mr Clayton and Marie Madelaine into town.'

'But I don't want to...'

Brad eased Blaze forward, caught the bridle of the girl's horse and drew her out of earshot of the rest.

'See here, Miss Renata, I ain't got time to waste arguin' with you. You ain't too old to have your bottom spanked if need be. You'll do as I say.'

The girl eyed him defiantly, her big hands clenching until the knuckles shone white, challenging him eyeball to eyeball until she realised he meant it.

'When you arrive, I want you to find this man's daughter, Victoria Clayton, and tell her what's happened. And at the same time, you'll not let this Frenchwoman outa your sight.'

'How can I do two things at once?' Renata said sullenly.

'It's a problem,' Brad agreed. 'But I'm sure you can handle it. There's somethin' else, too.' He took out his notebook and his brow furrowed for a few minutes as he scribbled a coded message to McNelly. He handed it to Renata. 'When you get into town, take that to the telegraph office pronto.'

'Will that be all?' Renata said sarcastically.

'Look,' Brad said. 'There's no call fer you to be uppity. I'm sorry if I was short with you just now. Believe me, I'm a busy man an' iffen you do what I'm askin' you're gonna make a real contribution to finding the man who killed your father.'

The girl shot him a doubtful look. 'OK – so long as I'm doing somethin' useful.'

'You bet you are,' Brad assured her. 'Now ride in nice'n easy with this buckboard an' do exactly as I've said.'

'I need someplace to bed down,' Renata said as they rejoined Tilson. 'Ma made it clear she wanted leavin' alone.'

'Here, take these.' Tilson handed her the keys to his office.

Brad waited while Renata had left and then set off back along the trail to the Lazy Z with Tilson cantering beside him.

'Renata seems to think those guys were lookin' fer somethin',' Tilson said. 'Any idea what that might be?'

'It was enough to make them nearly kill Joel Clayton. Maybe I'll get round to tellin' you soon,' Brad said.

They put their mounts to a steady canter until they reached the place where Brad had come upon Marie Madelaine and the wounded Clayton.

'We'll take a break. Brew some coffee. There's a can of beans in my saddlebag,' Brad said as they dismounted. 'I'll just take me a look around.'

Tilson did as he was asked. Whilst he coaxed up a small fire, he kept watching Brad out of the corner of his eye.

'Come and get it!' Tilson called out when he was ready.

When he had finished eating, Brad rolled a cigarette and exhaled a smoke ring into the heat haze. 'There were definitely four men here,' he opined.

Tilson stared at him. 'How can you be sure?'

'I read the sign,' Brad said laconically.

'But I thought only Indians could do that.'

'Then you've learned somethin'. There's enough evidence here to tell me that two men rode down the trail from the direction of Queensville, the other two came in from the brush. My guess is they split up. Way I figure it is two of 'em headed Clayton and Marie off, the other two blocked their retreat.'

'Very clever – but why?'

'I guess it's time you knew.' Brad fished in his vest pocket and pulled out the crumpled $20 note he had retrieved from the trail. He gave it to Tilson.

'Hold on to that,' he said while he produced a second uncreased note from his back pocket.

'Now hold 'em side by side,' he ordered.

Now that he knew what he was looking for, the difference in the number sizes stood out a country mile. Brad tapped the note Tilson was holding as he explained the difference.

Tilson stared at Brad. 'Are you saying Joel Clayton and Marie Madelaine are dealing in counterfeit money?'

'Right,' Brad said. 'And I reckon Colonel Valdez has grabbed the lot.'

Tilson's lips pursed in a whistle of disbelief. 'So that explains why Joel Clayton put up a fight. How much are we talkin' about?'

Brad rose and began to tread out the fire. 'That's what we gotta find out.'

'Wait a minute,' Tilson said, 'the other day you said that guy Johnson was some kinda government agent...'

'He was a detective workin' for the Treasury. He told me he'd been trailing counterfeit money for over a year. He was in the middle of tellin' me that Marie Madelaine was involved when he was shot. I figure he knew a good deal more about what was goin' on but he never got the chance to tell me.'

'Have you questioned Marie Madelaine?'

'I reckon she knows I'm onto her. Johnson told me she's a former Confederate spy. She's far too clever to give anythin' away.'

Tilson stroked his jaw reflectively. 'This business sounds a cut above bank robbin' and border rustlin'.'

'You're right, boy. My guess is that there's a whole heap of double-crossin' afoot. So far this business has cost the lives of Eli Johnson, Dan Jasper, a stage coach guard and Renata's father. I'll be very surprised if Joel Clayton lives to see another day. C'mon boy, we've got a whole heap of reasons to catch up with Colonel Valdez.'

After an hour of hard riding, Valdez reined in his mount and waited while the rest of his men gathered about him. To the west the Rio Grande lay coiled like a lazy snake, its water glistening as the sun climbed towards its zenith in a sky of washed out blue. He used his sombrero to fan away the dozens of thirsty flies which buzzed greedily around his sweating face.

'We are about half an hour's ride from the border,' he announced as he dismounted and unsaddled to allow his horse to roll. 'We will divide the money now, and then each man can go his own way. But make sure you keep clear of General Diaz' men. If you get caught with this money on you, you can expect no mercy.'

The men nodded assent as they unsaddled their mounts. They waited expectantly while Valdez paused to light a small cigar. They pressed in closer as he opened the first bag and plunged his hand inside.

As his hand withdrew a bundle of notes, Garcia led the whoops of delight.

'To hell with Diaz and the Revolution!' he shouted.

'I am rich at last!' the fat Manuel rubbed his pudgy hands together as he watched Valdez tip the first saddle bag over and shake out the tightly packed bundles onto the ground.

His beatific smile turned to horror with the rest of them and he stared in disbelief as Valdez clawed at the pile and picked up one of the neatly tied bundles, his face purple with rage.

'Paper! Worthless paper!' Valdez' voice cracked with emotion as he hurled the bundle back to the ground.

Garcia shouldered him aside and snatched up the second bag. The result was the same, clearly the top bundles in the mouth of each of the saddlebags were banknotes, the rest were bundles of paper. Garcia counted one of the bundles of notes.

'All we have is two thousand dollars for our trouble,' he said.

'She has duped me again!' Valdez muttered like a man possessed.

'So, the woman still has the money,' Garcia said softly.

'We have not finished with her yet. They were heading for Senor Clayton's ranch,' Valdez said. 'They should be there by now.'

'But there are only four of us,' Garcia

154

objected. 'The ranch hands will outnumber us by five to one.'

Valdez nodded. 'No doubt that is why they were fleeing there. The Lazy Z is well fortified. We are only two hours' ride from the camp. We will ride back and tell General Diaz we need more men to deal with this double-crossing *gringo*.'

Garcia stared at Valdez for a moment. Then he burst out laughing. 'Ask General Diaz for more men! Why, *senor*, you are as cunning as a fox!'

The sun was hot even though it was standing half-mast in the afternoon sky when after two hours of riding Brad spotted the discarded bundles of paper.

'What's with all this trash?' Tilson exclaimed disgustedly.

Brad dismounted and made a thorough investigation of the site. When he had finished, he squatted on his haunches and beckoned to Tilson to join him.

'Well, what do you make of it?' he asked the youngster as he crafted a smoke.

Tilson squatted beside him, a mystified look on his face.

'I'm baffled,' he said. 'How the devil you tracked 'em this far beats me.' He stared at the pile of bundles Brad had collected. 'What the hell is all this about?'

'I guess they don't talk about sleuthin' in the law books,' Brad said with a sigh.

'So what's goin' on?' Tilson demanded.

'Cutting sign is a hard learned specialty,' Brad told him. 'Figuring the significance of evidence is another. Look around at what you see and think.'

Tilson did as he asked.

'OK – what usually comes in bundles like that?' Brad asked him.

'Banknotes?'

'Sure – it looks as though Marie Madelaine has fooled the lot of us.'

Tilson stared at Brad. 'You mean she has the money back there with her?'

Brad exhaled a cloud of tobacco smoke and nodded.

'Marie Madelaine is a very clever woman,' he reflected. 'Too clever for her own good for I believe that she's now in greater danger than she's ever been.'

'You reckon Valdez will go after her again?'

'As sure as fate, he will.'

Brad arranged the bundles in a neat pile and counted them off. He stared reflectively. 'If this matches with what she's hidin' my guess is she's carryin' a hundred grand,' he said.

Tilson gasped. 'A hundred grand!'

'With money like this at stake, there's no way Valdez is gonna quit,' Brad said. He ground out the butt of his cigarette with his heel. 'Human nature don't allow that kind of thing.'

'But I don't get it, Valdez is ridin' with Diaz. What would Diaz want with a hundred grand in counterfeit money?'

'Exactly,' Brad cut in smoothly.

'You said earlier you thought it was destined for General Diaz. What use would he have for a hundred grand in counterfeit money?'

'None whatsoever,' Brad agreed. 'Maybe someone wanted him to get it...'

'Believin' it was genuine?'

Brad nodded.

Tilson stared at Brad. 'You mean someone is fittin' General Diaz up?'

'That's about the size of it.'

'But if he used counterfeit money to buy arms and supplies and it was traced back to him he'd be in deep trouble with our government.'

'Which would surely put paid to his plans fer a revolution,' Brad remarked.

Tilson digested this. 'So the Mexican

Government must be behind this?'

Brad nodded. Grudgingly he had to admit he was grateful for Tilson's penetrating questions. What the boy lacked in raw experience he made up for with a razor-sharp brain. Victoria was right, one day he'd make a mighty fine lawyer, a judge – maybe even State Governor – if he could stay alive.

'But what I don't understand is why Valdez is wantin' to take it by force.'

Brad ground out the butt of his cigarette carefully with his heel. 'Maybe he figures he'll find a private use fer it.'

Tilson pondered. 'D'you reckon Valdez thinks it's genuine?'

Brad thought for a moment. 'I ain't sure 'bout that yet, but I aim to find out. Now quit askin' questions and let's ride.'

'Which way d'you reckon they're headin'?' Tilson asked as they mounted their horses.

'Back towards the Lazy Z,' came the reply.

'So we'd best get after them,' Tilson said.

After half an hour's riding, Tilson reined in. 'Brad, I know you take me for a greenhorn, but we're ridin' due east, even I know there's no way we're heading for the Lazy Z.'

'Didn't say we were,' came the laconic reply. 'I sent Marie Madelaine back to town

158

– and that's where we're heading. I only hope that she hasn't given Renata the slip.'

'I got it! You intend to use her as some kinda bait to draw in Valdez!' Tilson exclaimed.

Brad nodded. 'You got it, boy.'

'I think that the ranger has told you to keep watch over me?'

Renata's mouth dropped open in amazement at Marie's perspicacity.

The other woman laughed. 'You do not need to answer. I see by your face that I am right. Very well, but you do not need to worry, I have a contract to sing at the Black Joke, you have my word that I shall not leave town.'

The two women continued their ride into Queensville. As they entered a sidestreet, Renata enquired of a gawping youngster the whereabouts of the doctor's house.

'Why not drop me at the hotel, first?' Marie suggested.

'No way,' Renata said, mindful of the ranger's express instructions to keep an eye on her.

'If we go any further, I shall be recognised,' Marie said. 'That could be awkward for both of us.'

'Sure,' Renata agreed. 'So hide under the cover.'

Marie Madelaine turned to look at the heavy tarpaulin in the well of the buckboard. She eyed it with distaste.

'Go on, get under it,' Renata urged.

Marie hesitated.

'Like you just said,' Renata observed. 'If they see you an' me totin' Mr Clayton wounded, there's gonna be some awkward questions asked,' Renata said. 'If I'm on my own I can just say I found him out on the trail and I'm bringing him in.'

One or two people were already coming into view. Taking a deep breath. Marie turned round and wriggled underneath the noisome tarpaulin.

'I'll let you know when we reach the hotel,' the girl said with friendly slap on the cover.

She walked the buckboard round to Doc Jeffries' house.

'Joel Clayton?' The doctor's eyebrows lifted when he recognised his patient. 'A knife wound, I see. Looks like no one is safe around these parts any more.'

Renata did not let the buckboard out of her sight whilst the doctor with the aid of a couple of passers by lifted the injured man down and carried him into the house.

'Can you let his daughter know?' Renata asked Doc Jeffries.

'No problem, she's teaching at the school. I'll send a message round immediately,' he replied.

The first job done successfully, as she moved the buckboard on towards the plaza, Renata figured all the while how she was going to keep an eye on the woman hidden under the tarpaulin.

The solution came to her with all the clarity of a vision of the Holy Virgin.

'We'll soon be there!' she said in a loud voice, for Marie Madelaine's benefit. 'Hup, hup!' she cried and moved the buckboard at a smart trot away from the plaza.

A few moments later, she drew the buckboard level with the sheriff's office. Using the keys Tilson had given her, she unlocked the door. Then she returned to the buckboard, whipped back the tarpaulin and before the disorientated Marie Madelaine knew where she was, she was frog-marched through the office and straight into one of the cells.

The glow of a job well done flushed Renata's face as she banged the cell door shut and turned the key. She'd show this ranger guy and Tilson McCracken just what law-keeping was all about ... and the astonished look on Marie Madelaine's face made it even more worthwhile.

'This is the first time I have been in jail in my whole life. What game are you playing, *mademoiselle?*' Marie Madelaine demanded shrilly.

'Me, I ain't playin' no games,' Renata said. 'I aim to do exactly what the ranger told me. Which is take care of you.'

'Somebody must have seen you bringing me in here. When I do not come out, they will tell Jake Rauchtenbauer...'

Renata checked the action of her Winchester, laid it on the desk and seated herself behind it with the air of someone who knows she has completed a job well done.

'So, now we wait for Mr Rauchtenbauer,' she said.

Over at the Black Joke, Jake Rauchtenbauer pondered his latest turn of events. Fancy letting a guy like Clayton get a drop on him and get clean away! He must be losing his touch. But it looked like now he had the last laugh for the word was that Clayton had arrived at the doc's place knifed real bad and what was even more fantastic, that butch kid Renata had been seen frog-marching Marie

Madelaine into the sheriff's office. There was no sign of the ranger and his sidekick McCracken or Valdez.

What the hell was goin' on?

He thought of the hundred grand Marie was carrying and licked his lips. He'd guessed she and her brother were doing a deal with Clayton but he'd reckoned it would be more like the usual five or ten grand. The fact that she was going to sing at the refurbished Black Joke was the icing on his cake as far as he was concerned, for he had no quarrel with Joel.

But one hundred grand!

It would be easy to use it to finance a whole series of deals along the border. There would be no hurry – that was the way to do it. The dazzling prospect of becoming the biggest man on the south west border spread out before him. With Johnson out of the way it would take months for his successor to pick up the threads of the investigation. If things got too hot, he could always destroy what was left and cut himself out...

But what the hell was goin' on?

There was only one way to find out...

Scarcely twenty minutes elapsed before the door crashed open and Rauchtenbauer strode into the sheriff's office. Renata regarded him with equanimity.

Rauchtenbauer caught sight of Marie Madelaine sitting inside the cell and eyed Renata with an air of incredulous disbelief.

'What the hell is goin' on?' he demanded.

'You'd better ask Ranger Saunders that,' Renata said calmly.

Rauchtenbauer placed both hands on the desk and thrust his face forward aggressively. 'Now, see here, young lady, you best stop playin' games and let Miss Madelaine go free, otherwise you just might get your bottom slapped.'

'That's the second time I've had that promise today,' Renata said cheekily.

'The key.'

As Rauchtenbauer held out his hand he found himself staring into the barrel of the Winchester Renata had snatched up from the desk.

'I damn nearly killed you earlier today, mister,' she said softly. 'Now get the hell outa here before you make me regret I don't do it right now.'

Rauchtenbauer saw the glint in her eye as he backed off towards the door.

'You're crazy, plumb crazy!' he exclaimed as he disappeared into the street.

Victoria Clayton had just finished rapping the knuckles of a truculent red-haired nine year old with a wooden foot ruler when Pedro Gonzales appeared outside her class-room door.

'What do you want?' Victoria snapped as she opened the door to him. She didn't like punishing pupils but it had been a long, hard day and her patience was at the end of its tether. Pedro's smile revived her. He had always tried so hard at school, but had left last year without much success.

'*Con permiso por favor, senorita*, but I have a message for you.'

Victoria opened the note. She recognised Doc Jeffries' scrawl at once.

'*Your father has been badly wounded. He is presently at my house. Please come at once.*'

'What happened?' Victoria asked Pedro.

He shook his head. 'This I do not know. The *medico* he ask me to take care of his buckboard and horses. He ask me to bring you this note.' He leaned forward confiden-tially. 'It is said that the *Senorita* Marie Madelaine is in jail...'

Victoria dismissed her class hastily, slipped a shawl round her shoulders and hurried across the plaza to Doc Jeffries' house. The doctor was drying his hands as she entered his surgery. Her father was lying on the couch, his chest swathed in bandages.

'What happened?' she asked the doctor anxiously.

The doctor shook his head as he drew her outside the door. Once out of earshot he said, 'I'm doin' the best I can, Miss Victoria, but the lung was punctured by a knife blade. He's had a long ride into town with fluid building up all the time. Your father's a strong man, but he ain't young any more. I have to tell you, I can't see him lasting out much longer.'

'Have you any idea who did this?' she demanded. There was not a trace of a tear in her eyes as she stared at the doctor.

Doc Jeffries shook his head. 'Renata Orsini brought him in. I figure she found him out on the trail. It ain't my remit to ask why or how. I just do my job the best I can.'

Victoria nodded. Doc Jeffries was a highly respected man in the county. He'd spent more time patching up the consequences of man's inhumanity to man than most. Everyone trusted him, both honest man and outlaw for he never betrayed a confidence. As she moved towards the door he said, 'Miss Victoria, my surmise is that your father has gotten himself mixed up with somethin' he couldn't handle.'

'It's that woman, Marie Madelaine,' Victoria said. 'I told pa she was pure poison but he wouldn't listen. Can I have a word with him?'

'Sure, but go easy.'

Victoria re-entered the room and bent low over her father.

His eyes flickered open and his pale features broke into a wan smile.

'Vicky, I'm sure glad to see you.'

She grasped his hand. Her father was the only person in the world who ever called her Vicky. 'Don't you fret none, pa. You're gonna be OK. Doc Jeffries says so.'

Joel Clayton shook his head, almost imperceptibly. 'Don't lie to me, Vicky. You always were a good girl. A credit to your ma. As fer me, well I guess I've let you down real bad.'

'Oh pa! Don't say that...'

'It's true. I got mixed up in somethin' that was too big fer me.'

'Don't fret yourself, pa. Just take it easy. You ain't done nothing we can't sort out.'

'Vicky, I done wrong an' I gotta pay fer it. You're gonna inherit the Lazy Z. You've got more'n enough brains to do it, but I don't like it you should run that place on your own.'

Tears streamed down Victoria's face as she held her father's hand.

'Marry Tilson, Vicky. He's a good boy.'

For a moment, Victoria thought her father had fallen asleep, but suddenly he opened his eyes and said, 'Tell Tilson not to ruin his life lookin' fer who killed his pa.' Joel Clayton was growing weaker now. 'The guy who did it was...'

His voice sank so low that Victoria had to put her ear close to his mouth to pick up the name...

NINE

General Porfirio Diaz was poring over a map when an aide entered his tent to announce the arrival of Colonel Valdez.

'So, at last you have brought me the American money.'

There was a domineering expression in his hooded eyes as they swept over Colonel Valdez in a penetrating appraisal. A heavily-built man, dressed less flamboyantly than

168

his officers, General Diaz, in any other circumstances would have passed for a sly provincial lawyer.

Outside the tent there was a hoarse command followed by a ragged volley of rifle fire as the army of rebels went about the business of preparing for a revolution.

'No, General, I have not.'

'Colonel Valdez, you gave me your assurance that the money would come. We are badly in need of arms and supplies. Without them my army will melt away.'

'The American agent has stolen it.'

'What? Are you telling me our cause has been betrayed?' Diaz rose hastily as he spoke, knocking over a glass of wine as he did so, spilling the blood red contents across the map. 'You came to me with a firm promise that there was a hundred thousand dollars in aid from the American Government. I have contracts for arms and ammunition waiting to be signed on the strength of those promises.'

'Do not worry, General,' Valdez said smoothly. 'The double-crossing gringo who has it has gone into hiding not far from here.'

'So what are you waiting for?' General Diaz demanded.

'I have but four men. I am outnumbered.

Give me another twenty, I can bring it back to you before nightfall,' Valdez replied boldly.

'Do it!' Diaz snapped. 'But take care not to show your face here again until you have the money.'

It was late afternoon when Brad and Tilson rode into the dusty streets of Queensville. Both men stared in amazement when Renata, armed with her Winchester, opened the door of the sheriff's office to them.

'What the blazes are you doin' here?' Brad demanded.

As he stepped inside he caught sight of Marie Madelaine sitting in one of the cells and Victoria Clayton standing with her arms folded.

'What's goin' on?' Brad demanded.

'I stopped by at the doc's and left Mr Clayton with him,' Renata said. 'He sent a message to Miss Clayton.'

'How is your father?' Brad asked Victoria.

'I spoke to him for a few moments before he died,' Victoria said stonily.

Brad felt as though his innards had been touched with ice. Looking at Victoria's stricken face reinforced his determination to get to the bottom of this whole affair.

'I came here to find out what happened, but I'm not getting any answers,' Victoria said.

'As soon as I'm sure of the facts, you'll be the first to know,' Brad assured her. As he glanced across at the cell, his mouth dropped open when he saw Marie Madelaine.

'You told me to keep an eye on her,' Renata said. 'I figured this was the best place. When Mr Rauchtenbauer stopped by earlier on, he didn't agree.'

'I'll bet he didn't,' Brad replied. Inside he felt elated at the girl's clear-headed initiative.

'Send for Pedro to take the horses to the livery barn an' keep your eyes skinned,' he told Tilson. 'My guess is Valdez will be back fer a showdown. The minute you see somethin' suspicious, let me know.'

'I'll brew some coffee,' Renata said.

'Ladies, if I read this situation right, it's gonna get mighty dangerous hereabouts very soon. We gotta get you all outa here before Valdez returns.'

As Brad approached the cell door, Marie Madelaine rose to meet him, a look of anger on her face.

'When are you going to let me out of this filthy place, Ranger Saunders? I demand to know!'

'That might depend on how soon you turn over the counterfeit money,' Brad replied, lowering his voice.

'Counterfeit money?' Marie's voice dropped to a whisper. 'I do not know what you are talking about, *monsieur.*'

'Oh come on, Marie,' Brad said wearily. 'Eli Johnson put you in the frame just before Valdez murdered him. The game's up, you've duped Valdez twice now.'

A cunning smile flickered across Marie's face. 'I think *monsieur* that perhaps you know too much. Be careful, for it has cost many a man his life before now.'

'I ain't surprised about that,' Brad agreed. 'Especially where you're involved.'

Marie came closer to the cell bars. As she brushed her breasts provocatively against them, Brad became aware of the intense sexual attraction her nearness afforded him.

'Listen, *monsieur,* you are right. When Valdez finds he has not got the money, he will come looking for me,' she whispered. 'There will be trouble for you if he finds I am here.'

Brad nodded. That was exactly what he had been thinking. Valdez must have checked out the Lazy Z and found Marie wasn't there. By now he should be well on his way to Queensville – no doubt with reinforcements. How could he defend the jail with three women and an inexperienced young sheriff to protect if Valdez chose to attack?

'The money is stitched in the lining of my dress,' Marie said.

'Was this money intended for General Diaz?'

Marie nodded.

'So why is Valdez tryin' to take it from you by force?'

'I think, *monsieur*, that he is a traitor to his country.'

Brad's mouth dropped open in disbelief. 'So Valdez is a Mexican Government agent, planted in Diaz' camp?' he said when he found his voice again.

'And now he works only for himself.'

'So, are you sayin' that Valdez intended not only to double-cross his own government, but also General Diaz, Joel Clayton – and your brother as well?'

Marie gave a low laugh. *'C'est la vie, monsieur.'*

'But then I guess you'd know all about that kinda thing, wouldn't you, Marie?' Brad said harshly.

'Ah, so you know I spied for the Confederacy?'

Brad nodded. 'Eli Johnson told me.'

Marie drew herself up haughtily. 'Do not compare me with scum like Valdez. I stayed true to the Confederate cause. But enough of that, I still have the money.'

'What are you sayin'?' Brad demanded.

'The day will come when I will be too old to sing. Maybe you too, will become too old to be a ranger?'

'It ain't a job I can do forever,' Brad admitted.

Marie's voice dropped even lower, her husky tone bewitching him. 'A man like you must have fought in the war.'

'Sure, I rode with Jeb Stuart.'

'My brother and I, we lost our estates, our wealth – everything. Now we take back what is ours and to hell with the Union!'

'With counterfeit money?'

Marie shrugged. 'Money is nothing but pieces of paper. Men fight for it, die for it...'

She leaned through the bars and caressed Brad's bristly cheek with her fingers.

'We are two of a kind, you and I. We spent the best years of our lives fighting for a lost cause. Take me out of town now. If we take fresh horses, Valdez and his men will never catch us. And when we reach Corpus Christie, I promise I will make it worth your while.'

When he hesitated, she caressed his face again. 'All through the war, Eli Johnson pursued me but he never caught me. I am like a seagull, I must fly free or I will die. The money means nothing. Take it and burn it if you wish. Only get me out of here, *cheri*. I will pay any price you ask.'

'I gotta think,' Brad muttered.

'Very well, *cheri*.' She blew him a kiss as he withdrew. 'But do not take too long about it.'

Brad left the cell and sat down at Tilson's desk, his brain awhirl with the things Marie had told him. Renata brought him a mug of coffee. As she set it down in front of him she said, 'A telegraph message has just arrived for you, Ranger Saunders.'

Brad ripped it open. It was from Captain McNelly himself.

'The Marquis de Bau heading for Queensville. Arrest on arrival.'

Brad tilted back his stetson and scratched his head. So the marquis was coming, no doubt to check up on the deal...

'You got a problem, Ranger Saunders?' Renata asked innocently.

Brad shot her an old-fashioned look. 'Sure, I got Valdez arrivin' any minute an' I got you, Miss Victoria an' Marie Madelaine

175

on my hands.'

Renata considered this for a moment. Then she said, 'Then why not let me take Miss Victoria and Marie Madelaine someplace else?'

Brad pondered. This girl had all the makings of another Calamity Jane. But her idea appealed to him. Why not let her keep charge of Marie Madelaine? After all she had done a good job so far.

As Renata picked up her Winchester, Brad noticed the easy way it sat in her big hands.

'The hotel she's stayin' at is just across the way. I could take her out the back way,' she offered. 'Once she's inside, there she stays. If she tries anythin' I'll blow her brains out.'

'What about Jake Rauchtenbauer?' Brad demanded. 'You said you'd had trouble from him earlier on...'

'Brad – there's a whole heap of riders leavin' the plaza and they're headin' this way!' Tilson called urgently from the doorway.

'OK. Unlock the cell and get Marie Madelaine and Victoria round to the hotel as fast as you can,' Brad ordered Renata.

He joined Tilson beside the door. Behind him he was aware of Marie Madelaine's furious protest followed by a sharp slap, a yelp of pain and a short scuffle as Renata and Victoria hustled their captive out of the back door.

'Now, see here, boy, you check your artillery while I parley with these guys,' Brad said to Tilson after the women had left the building. 'Iffen there's any trouble, you back me, ya hear?'

'I hear you,' Tilson said.

Brad noticed with satisfaction that the boy's hands were steady as he checked the first of his Le Mats.

As he stepped outside the office onto the boardwalk, to his intense relief Brad noticed that Tilson's mount together with Blaze had been taken away to safety. Valdez and three others had detached themselves from the company sized band of cutthroats filling the otherwise empty street. With a twinge of dismay his eye took in some twenty men gathered behind them. Valdez must have stopped by at Diaz' camp for reinforcements. They looked as rough a bunch of border bandits as he'd set eyes on. Was Diaz really going to try to take Mexico City with an army like this?

Valdez reined in twenty feet away from Brad.

'So, *senor*, I think maybe that you and I meet at last,' he said haughtily.

'So what brings you here?' Brad replied.

'Oh I think you know that very well, *senor*. You have inside there the woman Marie Madelaine.'

'So what?'

Valdez' expression changed. His face assumed an expression of satanic fury. 'Do not play poker with me, *senor*. I have wasted enough time already at the Lazy Z ranch. I have here with me a company of soldiers. The woman, she has money belonging to General Diaz. She must hand it over to me immediately.'

'And if she doesn't?'

Even as he spoke, Brad saw the hand of one of Valdez' henchmen inching towards his sidearm.

Valdez spread his arms wide in a gesture of resignation. 'We will have to take it by force.'

But Brad wasn't listening. Could he rely on young Tilson? Did he have the nerve to back him up?

But before he could react to Valdez' henchman's stealthy movement, there was a great boom from behind him. The man's gun slipped from his hand and he slumped forward dead in the saddle, shot through the heart by a slug from one of Tilson's Le Mats.

Suddenly all hell was let loose in the Street

as Tilson charged forward with a mighty shout. Brad watched in horror as the young sheriff took his stance four-square in the middle of the dusty street blazing away with both of the Le Mats, cursing and shouting like a madman as he emptied the nine shot chambers into the mass of rearing horses and men. Taking his cue, Brad drew his own weapon, shooting calmly, picking targets, making every shot count ruthlessly until his Peacemaker was empty.

'Get inside, boy!' he shouted at Tilson.

The pair of them dived for the door to the office under cover of a rolling cloud of dust and gunsmoke.

Once inside, Brad slammed the door shut and dropped the heavy bar into place.

'Don't you ever do that again, boy!' he shouted at Tilson. 'Not if you wanna live to tell the tale.'

But Tilson had the red raw lust of battle in his eyes as he reloaded his Le Mats. Brad held his arm with all his strength to restrain him but failed to prevent him from smashing a hole in one of the barred windows.

'Let them come!' he snarled as he pointed one of the Le Mats down the street.

'Hold your fire, boy, they ain't there no more,' Brad said calmly.

As Tilson drew back, Brad peered out to see a horse cantering down the street carrying its dead rider slumped like a broken puppet in the saddle. The front of the sheriff's office looked like a battlefield with the bodies of men and horses strewn everywhere. Brad counted six corpses and four dead horses in the carnage. But there was no sign of Valdez in the now empty Street.

'I'm sorry, Brad,' Tilson gasped as he slumped by the wall. 'I guess I got fightin' mad.'

Brad ducked as a fusillade of shots smashed against the woodwork, one smashed a window pane showering them both with glass.

Brad laid back against the wall and advanced slowly so he could take another look down the street. No one was in sight either way, Valdez must have dispersed his remaining men, no doubt with the intention of surrounding the jail. They were already on the roof of the building opposite, he could tell by the angle of entry of the slugs which smashed into the wooden floor.

'You reckon they'll rush us?' Tilson asked.

'Naw, I reckon we gave them a bellyful.'

Even as he spoke, a cart came into view. To his horror, Brad saw it was full of hay and being pushed towards them. Smoke and flames rose from a torch carried by one man.

'I was wrong, they are gonna smoke us out,' Brad shouted to Tilson. 'Check your weapons and make every shot count.'

Renata and Victoria made their escape from the rear of the jail with Marie Madelaine sandwiched between them.

'Now, you stay close to me and you say nothing,' Renata muttered as they emerged into the plaza.

Walking perfectly normally side by side, the three women arrived at the hotel. The clerk handed over the key, his eyes too bemused by the beauty of Marie Madelaine to notice the other two. Once inside the room, Renata locked the door.

'You are making a big mistake,' Marie Madelaine said to Renata as she poured a glass of wine. She offered it to Victoria but she refused. 'Colonel Valdez will attack the jail, thinking I am still there. The ranger and your friend, they will be killed and then when it's over, Valdez will find I am not there and then he will come looking for me.'

Even as she spoke there was a crackle of firing from the direction in which they had come.

'The fighting has started already,' Marie said with a sorrowful shake of the head. 'It is a pity the young sheriff will die.' She gave Renata a sly look. 'I think he liked you.'

Renata did not reply. She walked over to the window and looked outside. Victoria joined her.

'What does she mean when she says Tilson liked you?' she said accusingly.

Renata flushed. 'Nothing, I guess she's out to make trouble between us,' she said.

'But you like him, I guess?' Victoria pressed her.

'OK so I'm not a looker like you. What does it matter, there's no way he'll ever take a shine fer the likes of me!' Renata retorted. She cradled her Winchester in her arms. 'Look, I reckon we're wastin' time both of us being here. Why don't you stay here with Marie Madelaine and I'll go take a look outside? There may be somethin' I can do to help those guys inside the jail.'

When Victoria looked doubtful, Renata passed her the handcuffs. 'Fasten her to the bed with those, that should keep her quiet.'

As Renata closed the door, Victoria approached Marie with the intention of carrying out her suggestion. But as she drew close she was taken completely by surprise by Marie's frenzied attack which left her bruised and bleeding and handcuffed to the head of the bedstead herself.

Jake Rauchtenbauer slipped out of the Black Joke by the rear entrance. Word had already spread of Valdez' abortive attack on the sheriff's office. One of his hired muscle had also reported seeing Marie Madelaine walking across to the hotel in the company of Renata Orsini and Victoria Clayton.

He eased the gunbelt carrying his trusty Smith & Wesson. Three women was about as many as he could handle, he thought with a grin. While Valdez was laying his fruitless siege to the sheriff's office, he would take this heaven-sent opportunity to release Marie Madelaine. No doubt she would be more than willing to trade her freedom for the vast amount of money she was carrying.

He strode across the deserted plaza towards the main entrance to the hotel, banking on the fact that the eyes of the townsfolk would be focussed on events at the sheriff's office.

'Is Miss Madelaine in her room?' he asked the desk clerk with a smile as he entered the lobby.

'Yes, sir,' came the reply.

Rauchtenbauer took the stairs two at a time. When he arrived outside the door, he listened for a moment before knocking.

'Who is it?'

He recognised Victoria's voice.

'It's me, Jake Rauchtenbauer,' he said. 'Open up, Victoria, I got some news.'

'I can't.'

Rauchtenbauer stood back, puzzled. What did she mean saying she couldn't open the door? He pondered for a moment and then tried again. With the same result.

He stood back and thought hard. If he had a dollar for every time he'd asked himself what the hell was going on he'd be a rich man before the day was out.

Suddenly he made his mind up. Standing back, he shoulder charged the door. The woodwork was stronger than the lock which burst open and sent him staggering into the room. His eyes widened as he saw Victoria handcuffed to the bed.

As his eyes swept the room, he realised she was alone. He gave a lop-side grin. Life afforded some strange spectacles, but none so strange as the spectacle of Victoria Clayton, the high and mighty schoolmistress, handcuffed to the bed as one of his honky tonks was occasionally by one of his kinkier minded clients.

Victoria shrank away when she saw him, seeing the lust raging in his eyes.

'Well, now, ain't it just my lucky day!' Rauchtenbauer exclaimed.

As he advanced on Victoria the click of the door closing behind him made him whirl round, his hand diving for his Smith & Wesson.

'Don't even think of it, mister.'

'Not you again!' he exclaimed as Renata approached him, her Winchester pointing at his belly.

'I saw you headin' this way and figured you were up to no good,' Renata said.

She produced the keys from her pocket and tossed them to Rauchtenbauer. 'Unlock those cuffs.'

Rauchtenbauer did as she ordered.

'I guess Miss Madelaine was too smart for you,' Renata remarked to Victoria when she was free.

'Ranger Saunders won't be too pleased when he hears about it,' Victoria agreed. 'In the meantime, this guy is my prisoner and no way is he gonna escape.'

'Now wait a minute,' Rauchtenbauer protested. 'There's no way I'm staying here with you two.' He spread his hands wide. 'What am I supposed to have done?'

'We'll see about that,' Victoria said grimly.

'I've had enough of this nonsense,' Rauchtenbauer growled.

He brushed past Victoria and made a dash for the door. As he did so, Renata stuck her foot out bringing him down like a roped steer. As he fell, his head smashed against the corner of the oak dressing table.

'Out cold,' Renata gave her verdict as she bent over him and snapped the handcuffs onto his wrists. 'Keep an eye on him, and I'll send Tilson across to collect him.'

TEN

Renata went downstairs and, openly carrying her rifle, walked past the open-mouthed lobby clerk.

Out in the street, she headed for the plaza and crossed it heading towards the sheriff's office. It was the siesta and after the cool interior of the hotel, the sun's heat struck her with the intensity of an oven. As she went, Renata was conscious of faces peering through the windows and low voices muttering as she walked past the clapboard frontages. There was a tension in the atmosphere reflecting the citizens' telepathic awareness that something momentous was happening.

Renata reached the boardwalk at the entrance to the street and paused. A shiver ran down her spine when she saw the corpses of dead men and horses. It was plain that Tilson and the ranger had put up a fierce resistance. They must be still alive for there was still a large number of rebel soldiers, carefully keeping clear of the field of fire from the sheriff's office. Ahead of her a fat, sweating Mexican was standing guard, armed with a rifle held at high port and crossed bandoliers stuffed with enough cartridges to fight a major battle. He was standing with his back towards Renata, watching impassively as his *compadres* further down the street gathered round a cart stashed high with hay.

Please God let Valdez be there! she prayed as she melted into the deep shadow of the boardwalk. She dropped to her hands and knees and crawled forward keeping out of sight of the sentry.

Valdez was there!

At a distance of a hundred yards, her keen eyes picked his tall figure out moving amongst his men, issuing orders, castigating their incompetence with a stream of blasphemy.

She watched, puzzled.

What were they about to do?

As Renata strained to see, Valdez and his men began to advance on the sheriff's office under the cover of the cart. Smoke and flames rose from a torch wielded by one of the men.

The Mexicans were about to smoke Tilson and the ranger out!

The sight of the flames from the torch brought back all the horror of her father's death. In Renata's mind Valdez became a monster, obsessed with fire.

Her brain became ice cold as she raised the Winchester and went down on one knee. The range was no problem. Out of sight of the guard, she rested the barrel on the rail of the boardwalk, tucked the butt firmly into her shoulder and took sight on the tall, broad shoulder figure of Valdez. The first time she had aimed at a human target, she had missed. This time, she would not fail. She tracked his movement just as she would a rabbit, holding the weapon lightly but firmly. Just as she was ready to pull the trigger a shot rang out from behind her...

'Hold your fire,' Brad ordered Tilson as the cart drew closer.

'We ain't got a chance,' Tilson raged. 'I'm gonna open that door and rush them.'

'Hold it boy.' It took all Brad's strength to prevent Tilson from surging forward to the attack.

The cart drew nearer and stopped. Out in the street the silence was almost tangible until Valdez' voice rose in a shout.

'Are you coming out, *senor* or do I have to burn you out?'

When there was no reply, Valdez shouted again, 'Come on out *senor*. I know the women have left. My men are searching the town. It is only a matter of time before they find them.'

Brad turned round to face Tilson, his gun held high. He glanced at the gun case. 'I don't usually care to tote more'n one gun, but throw me another Colt, Tilson.' He checked the action and loaded it rapidly.

'It looks as if you're right, Tilson boy, we're gonna have to charge our way outa this. When I give the word, we get outside take 'em by surprise an' let 'em have all the firepower we got.'

He walked to the door. As he eased it open, the cart appeared in full view, massively concealing the chattering, indisciplined rabble of men behind it.

'*Hágalo!*' Valdez' voice rose in a harsh command.

As the cart loomed closer, a single shot rang out.

'Let's go!' Brad shouted.

He and Tilson emerged from the door and fanned out left and right to enfilade the men sheltering behind the cart, their guns blazing in unison after they had bellied down onto the boardwalk.

As Brad emptied the last chambers of his weapons, he clawed at his gunbelt to reload as fast as he could. On his right Tilson was doing the same.

Suddenly he realised that there was no return fire, yet the street was full of riders, surging in from both ends, finally coming together and milling around in front of them.

'It's General Diaz!' Tilson shouted. 'It looks like he brought his whole damn army with him!'

Suddenly the riders parted to allow their general through. As Brad stepped forward, his ragged appearance stood out in marked contrast to the general's finery. He holstered his Peacemaker and shoved the second weapon into his belt.

'What brings you here, General?' he asked. 'The agreement was that you keep your men close to the border and within the confines of your camp.'

General Diaz stared at Brad, contempt in his hooded eyes.

'I do not think, *senor* that you are in a position to stop me,' he said softly.

Brad flipped back his vest; as he did so, he was conscious of dozens of pairs of eyes focussing on his silver star.

'*Los Diablos Tejanos!*'

As the hated words flashed from mouth to mouth, Brad was aware of Tilson standing behind him. Would the boy keep his nerve in front of men who hated the guts of Texans and regarded the rangers with impotent fury.

'Captain McNelly sent me here,' Brad said. 'He will expect me to return.'

As General Diaz gave an imperceptible nod, Brad felt relief rising inside him. Behind the general, his men were clearing the street of corpses. One of them led a horse carrying one of them in front of the general.

'It's Valdez!' Tilson muttered.

'So, I have what I came for,' General Diaz said to Brad. 'I think now that we will return to camp. *Hasta la vista, senor.*'

He wheeled his horse round and his men

formed up in a long ragged column behind him as he led the way out of town.

'Hell!' Tilson exclaimed. 'I didn't realise that badge of yours could turn back a whole army.'

As he spoke, two people emerged from the settling dust clouds. They were walking on foot.

'It's Victoria!' Tilson exclaimed as he stepped into the street watching the strange little procession. 'An' she's got Jake Rauchtenbauer with her!'

As they drew closer, Brad and Tilson moved out to meet them. Other citizens, sensing the drama was over began to appear in the street.

To Brad's amazement, he saw that Rauchtenbauer was handcuffed and being prodded along by the Smith & Wesson in Victoria's hand. He seemed dazed and as he drew closer Brad saw his hair was matted with blood from a blow to the head.

'This is the man who shot Tilson's father,' Victoria said. 'I've put him under arrest.'

Tilson started forward. 'What the hell,' he snarled, raising one of his reloaded Le Mats.

Brad stepped forward and knocked Tilson's gun arm down with numbing force.

'Hold it!' he commanded. 'So what gives?'

he asked Victoria.

'My father told me the truth just before he died,' she replied. 'He said Jake Rauchtenbauer had murdered Abe McCracken. He said he didn't want Tilson to waste his life chasin' his father's killer.'

'That's a lie!' Rauchtenbauer exclaimed as Brad and Tilson hustled him into a cell. His knuckles turned white as he grasped the bars of his cell. 'She's fittin' me up so she can get back in with Tilson,' he shouted.

'No way,' Brad rapped. 'Why should Miss Victoria put the finger on you? She knows nothing about your past. Nobody does. That's what you were gamblin' on when you set yourself up in business at the Black Joke. Well mark this, a dying man's word is gonna be enough to hang you, Rauchtenbauer. So where is Marie Madelaine?' Brad asked Victoria, abruptly changing the subject. 'I thought I told you and Renata to keep an eye on her.'

'I guess she fooled the pair of us,' Victoria said.

Brad's face turned grim. 'You mean you let her get away?' he said bitterly.

'Ah, *monsieur*, my sister is too clever for all of you.'

They turned to face a tall man, elegantly

dressed to the point of dandyism. Not a speck of dust soiled his neat grey suit. His waxed moustache, curling upwards, gave the impression that he was wearing a permanently fixed smile.

'Who the, hell are you?' asked Tilson incredulously.

'I am the Marquis de Bau,' the newcomer said. He caressed his silky black beard. 'I wouldn't do that, *messieurs*, if I were you,' the man warned as both Brad and Tilson's hands strayed towards their guns.

In view of the Colt Patent House Pistol the marquis was holding, to obey seemed the wisest course.

Rauchtenbauer stepped forward to the bars of his cell, his expression jubilant. 'Glad you came along, Marquis. Now let me outa here...'

The smile froze on his face as the pistol barked. Brad and Tilson watched in amazement as Rauchtenbauer coughed blood and toppled forward onto the floor of the cell.

'I will not work with incompetent fools,' the marquis said contemptuously as he blew away the wisp of smoke from the barrel of his gun.

'You just killed him in cold blood!' Tilson shouted.

'Hold it, boy,' Brad grabbed Tilson by the arm and restrained him. 'If he did it to him, he'll do it to you.'

'You are very wise, *monsieur*,' the marquis said.

'Seems like you win, Marquis,' Brad said. 'I guess you'll be pleased to know your sister still has the money. Best not show your face in Texas fer a long time. We rangers have long memories.'

The marquis pushed open the door of the cell and indicated for Brad and Tilson to enter it.

'I am aware of that, *monsieur*. Which is the reason, why I want you and your friend out of the way while I and my sister make our escape.'

Tilson eyed the marquis with distaste. 'What makes you think you'll get away from here? The rangers will track you wherever you go.'

'Over the sea, *monsieur*?' the marquis laughed. 'I have a boat waiting in the harbour. Fair stands the wind for France! My sister is already on board.' He removed a gold watch from his vest pocket, inserted a monocle in his right eye and consulted it. 'It is due to leave in ten minutes precisely. It will take us both out to a ship waiting in the bay.'

195

Brad and Tilson entered the cell. The marquis closed the door and turned to pick up the keys from the desk.

'Hold it right there, mister!'

The marquis froze.

'Renata!' Tilson exclaimed.

The Colt never wavered in the girl's grasp as she pointed it at the marquis.

'Let them out of the cell and you go inside,' she rapped. *Do it or I'll blow you apart!*

'You took your time, young lady,' Brad said as he emerged from the cell. 'Tilson, you take care of things here. I gotta get down to the harbour and catch up with Marie Madelaine.'

It was a forlorn hope, Brad knew as he ran out of the office with giant strides. Commandeering a loose horse, he leapt into the saddle and galloped along the narrow streets leading to the harbour.

He dismounted and paused, scanning the handful of fishing boats tied to the quay but there was no sign of anyone. He walked forward, puzzled. Where the hell was this boat the marquis was talking about?

'You lookin' fer the *Aurora*, mister?'

A grizzled old sea-dog emerged from the low doorway of a cottage. He limped towards Brad, carrying a half-gutted fish in his hand, a quizzical expression on his face which was as gnarled as the seasoned oak of a clipper's main mast.

'Could be,' Brad muttered.

'She's standing out to sea, over yonder.'

Out on the horizon, Brad saw the solitary ship, her snow white canvas billowing against the blue sky. For one brief nostalgic moment it reminded him of a wagon rolling along a wide prairie.

'Have a look through this.' The old timer passed him a spy glass. 'Take a look, young 'un. Ain't she beautiful? When steam finally takes over the sea will never be the same again.'

As Brad focused the instrument on the ship, a solitary figure leaning over the rail leapt into view.

The image was small but there was no mistake – it was Marie Madelaine! The distance was too far but he swore he could see her ironic smile as the ship receded from him. She must have seen him for she raised a hand to salute. As she did so, it seemed as though the air was full of fluttering paper.

The money! Brad shook his head in disbelief. Marie Madelaine was throwing away the evidence...

'The woman was picked up by a longboat.

She seemed to be waiting for someone else to come, but he never showed. 'Time and tide wait fer no man, I guess,' the old sea-dog volunteered with a sly glance at Brad.

Brad snapped the instrument shut and, as he turned away, the air rustled with the wings of a gull as it landed on the rail of a nearby fishing boat. Its beak opened and the bird filled the tiny harbour with its harsh, clattering, mocking cry.

'Ranger Saunders, I wanted to tell you how we lost Marie Madelaine,' a voice said behind him.

Brad turned to face Renata. She was sat awkwardly astride a horse that was too big for her. 'I told you to keep an eye on her,' he said harshly. He pointed out into the bay. 'Now she's on board yonder ship, bound for France.'

The girl hung her head.

'Mind you,' Brad conceded. 'If you hadn't turned up back there, the marquis would have been on board, too.'

Brad mounted his horse. He looked keenly at the girl. 'Ain't you got somethin' else to tell me?' he asked.

'Like what?'

'Someone back there picked off Valdez. Whoever did it broke up the Mexicans' attack before it even started. They saved my life and Tilson's, too.'

A strange light came into the girl's eyes. For a moment Brad thought she was going to speak but suddenly she whirled her horse round and galloped off.

Victoria Clayton greeted Brad with a frosty smile as the maid ushered him into the parlour of the Grand Palace Hotel. Earlier that afternoon they had buried Joel Clayton, but now the mourners had gone and she was standing with Tilson beside her, twisting his black hat in his huge hands, his expression sheepish.

'Ranger Saunders, could you possibly spare a few minutes to talk some sense into Tilson?'

Brad winced inwardly. During this last two days, Victoria Clayton had assumed the mantle of her late father's responsibilities as well he thought she would. She had accepted his explanation of events without question. As far as she was concerned, her father had fallen victim to human frailty and he had paid for it with his life. That was the way of the west. There was no doubt in Brad's mind that she would pick up the pieces and with suitable help would run her late father's ranching interests purposefully and well. But he figured he knew what was coming...

'Do you remember that conversation we had the day we first met?' Victoria demanded. 'Do you remember how I begged you to persuade Tilson not to be a lawman?'

'I guess so,' Brad replied.

'A fat lot you've done to help me,' Victoria retorted. 'Since then there's been nothing but shootin' and killin' and more of the same. And what's more, it seems like Tilson's developed a taste fer it. He's figurin' on movin' up a notch and joinin' you rangers.'

'I've learned a lot since I worked with you, Brad,' Tilson said with quiet conviction. 'I figure if I join the rangers I can do my bit to bring law and order to this part of Texas.'

'Gunlaw!' Victoria exclaimed. 'What kind of law is that?'

Brad cleared his throat. 'Listen, Tilson. Victoria is right. What Texas needs is law. An' by that I mean proper law, where men are given a fair trial in front of a jury and justice is seen to be done. Think about your future. What kinda land do you want your children to grow up in? Texas is long on men who figure they can handle a gun, but mighty short of young fellas who are men enough to use their brains to help build the kinda land we all want to live in.'

Tilson stared at Brad, respect evident in his frank blue eyes. 'Why Brad, I ain't never heard you talk this way before,' he said.

'I guess no one ever has before,' Brad replied. 'But my advice to you would be to throw in your sheriff's badge and get yourself qualified as a lawyer.'

'I can't do that,' Tilson said darkly. 'Not while my father's killer is still alive.'

'He wouldn't believe me when I told him my father said it was Jake Rauchtenbauer,' Victoria said despairingly.

'Your father's killer is dead,' Brad said quietly. 'Ranger Miller always suspected it was Jake Rauchtenbauer, but I would not reveal that until I was certain. Victoria's father has confirmed it. You can check the facts at HQ if you wish, it's all there in Ranger Miller's report.'

Victoria clasped Tilson's arm. 'Are you hearin' this man?' she cried.

'I hear him,' Tilson replied.

Victoria slipped her arm in his. 'Then there's no more need for you to search for your father's killer. I'll hire a good foreman to run the Lazy Z. You've only your finals to do. As soon as you're qualified we'll get married.'

Brad said, 'Once the federal agents have

collected the marquis there ain't no earthly reason for you to stay on as sheriff. Do as Miss Victoria says and one day I reckon you'll make a mighty fine judge. The kinda judge people will talk of with respect. That's what Texas needs. Think about it, Tilson. Your pa was proud of you. Don't you reckon that's what he always wanted?'

'And your mother does, too!' Victoria exclaimed.

For a few moments Brad was aware of turmoil in the youngster's mind.

'OK,' Tilson said suddenly. 'Maybe I wanted to be sheriff fer all the wrong reasons.'

'Tilson! Oh Tilson! I knew you'd see the sense of it!' Victoria exclaimed as she threw her arms round his neck and kissed him.

'Say now, there's no need to take on this way,' Tilson said with a look of intense embarrassment.

As Brad strode towards the door, Victoria broke away from Tilson and followed him. The mourners had long since gone and the still warm evening sun was standing on the horizon like a great red blood orange as he unhitched Blaze and threw his leg over the saddle.

Victoria stood arm-in-arm with Tilson in

the deep violet shadow of the stoop and watched Brad as he made ready to go.

'It's gettin' late, Brad. There ain't no cause fer you to leave now,' Victoria said. 'Why not stay the night here at the hotel? Have the best suite on the house.'

Brad thought of Johnson toppling forward across the desk. It might have been him, one day maybe, it would be him, cut down by an outlaw's bullet.

'I guess not,' he said. He leaned forward and patted Blaze on the neck. 'There's an hour of light left. I'll camp out on the range and lay me a few of my own plans. Now, Tilson, you make sure you keep that fancy Frenchman under lock and key until someone comes to collect him.'

'You bet I will!' Tilson exclaimed.

Marie Madelaine was right. It was good to be free. Despite the trouble she had caused, Brad felt a strange sense of loss that she had eluded him. Would she ever return to America? Somehow he knew she would. For America was the Land of the Free. Another place, another time, another name; women like Marie Madelaine were like the spirit of the universe, incomprehensible, enigmatic, unattainable.

'*We are two of a kind, you and I.*'

Words he would always remember.

'C'mon, Blaze, I'm gettin' sentimental,' he muttered.

Blaze thought so too, for the big bay kept up a bone rattling canter in tune with his mood. As the evening shadows lengthened, the sun-warmed earth seemed to exhale the very breath of life...

The light patter of hooves behind him disturbed his reverie and made him turn in the saddle.

'Hey, wait fer me!'

Brad stared as Renata drew alongside him.

'What are you doin' out here at this time?' he demanded.

'You ridin' to Corpus?' the girl replied with a question.

'What if I am?'

'That's where I wanna be. Ma's fixed up with her cousin here in Queensville. I reckon she'll marry him soon. She don't need me around. I reckon it's time I spread my wings. I got an uncle who's willin' to offer me work in his shipping company in New Orleans.'

'So what's wrong with the stage?'

The girl shrugged. 'I figured I'd be safer ridin' with you.'

Brad eyed the Winchester tucked in the

girl's scabbard. 'I reckon you can look after yourself.'

The girl looked wistful. It was plain to Brad that she'd changed. Suddenly it dawned on him – the fiery tomboy obsessed with revenge had matured into a woman. That was the way of things on the frontier.

'Mind if I ask you somethin'?' Brad said later as they sat round the camp fire eating bacon and beans.

'Go ahead,' the girl said.

'Did you fall for Tilson?'

She flushed as red as the embers she was stirring with a stick of mesquite. 'You figured that?'

'It was plain enough.'

'Maybe,' she replied with a shrug. A gleam appeared in her eye. 'OK, mister. Mind if I ask you 'bout Marie Madelaine?'

The publishers hope that this book has given you enjoyable reading. Large Print Books are especially designed to be as easy to see and hold as possible. If you wish a complete list of our books please ask at your local library or write directly to:

Dales Large Print Books
Magna House, Long Preston,
Skipton, North Yorkshire.
BD23 4ND

This Large Print Book, for people
who cannot read normal print,
is published under the auspices of

THE ULVERSCROFT FOUNDATION